TORCHWOOD

BAY OF
THE DEAD

Mark Morris

BOOKS

2 4 6 8 10 9 7 5 3 1

Published in 2009 by BBC Books, an imprint of Ebury Publishing
A Random House Group company

Torchwood is a BBC Wales production for BBC One
Executive Producers: Russell T Davies and Julie Gardner

The Random House Group Limited Reg. No. 954009.
Addresses for companies within the Random House Group can be found at
www.randomhouse.co.uk

A CIP catalogue record for this book is available from the British Library.

ISBN 978 1 846 07737 1

The Random House Group Limited supports The Forest Stewardship
Council (FSC), the leading international forest certification organisation.
All our titles that are printed on Greenpeace approved FSC certified paper
carry the FSC logo. Our paper procurement policy can be found at
www.rbooks.co.uk/environment

Commissioning Editor: Albert DePetrillo
Series Editor: Steve Tribe
Production Controller: Phil Spencer

Cover design by Lee Binding @ Tea Lady © BBC 2009
Typeset in Albertina and Century Gothic
Printed in Great Britain by Clays Ltd, St Ives plc

For Alan and Max,
who love zombies even more than I do

'Mike's funny, isn't he?'

Joe Hargreaves glanced at his wife, Jackie, who was sprawled on the passenger seat next to him, bare feet tucked up under her thighs. She had kicked off the high heels which made her legs look fantastic, but which she always complained were crippling to wear, and had released the clip which had been holding her carefully sculpted hair in place all evening. Now, with her blue silk dress shimmering in the light from the dashboard and her mahogany hair tumbling about her shoulders, Joe thought she looked gorgeous. He smiled teasingly.

'Funnier than me?'

'Don't be daft.' She matched his smile with her own. 'Funniest man in the world, you are.'

His smile widened into a grin. 'It's a natural gift,' he said.

'Course,' she murmured nonchalantly, pretending to examine her fingernails, 'I meant funny peculiar, not funny ha-ha.'

He adopted an expression of mortification, and a voice to match. 'Oh, now I'm hurt. I'm cut to the quick.'

She arched an eyebrow. 'The quick? Where's that then?'

'Dunno,' he said, shrugging. 'Opposite the slow?'

They laughed together. It had been a good night. They had spent it visiting their best friends, Mike and Sue Roach, in Llandaff, and were now on their way home to Cowbridge, full of good food and – in Jackie's case – good wine, both of them buzzing from an evening of friendship, laughter and great conversation.

The night was chilly but clear, silvery moonlight edging the trees, fields and hills that rolled gently outwards on either side of the hard grey artery of the A48. During the day this was a busy road, but now, on the wrong side of eleven o'clock, the twin headlamps of cars heading back towards the bright lights of Cardiff were few and far between.

Cocooned in the susurrating warmth from the heater and serenaded by the mournful beauty of Elbow's music drifting from the car's sound system, Jackie felt her eyelids drooping closed. She knew that uncurling herself from her seat and stepping out into the cold when they got home would be doubly horrible if she allowed herself to fall asleep, but she didn't care; she was warm and cosy and tired, and right at this moment that was all that mattered.

She was three-quarters asleep, the soft roar of the engine and the swirling music becoming part of her dream, when Joe said, 'That's strange.'

Reluctantly she opened one eye. 'What is?'

'This fog. It's appeared from nowhere. Look at it. It's like a barrier. Weird.'

Jackie had slumped down in her seat. She struggled upright and peered out through the windscreen. Blinked.

'That *is* weird,' she said.

The fog, thick and grey and impenetrable, seemed to stretch in a perfectly straight line across the road ahead. It stretched, in fact, as far as the eye could see in either direction, a smoky wall that bisected the landscape to left and right before dissolving into the darkness.

Almost unconsciously, Joe slowed the car to a crawl.

'It *is* fog, I suppose?' said Jackie. 'It's not something… solid?'

'Course it's fog,' Joe snapped, then flashed her a look of apology. 'Sorry, love, it's just… I'm a bit freaked by it, that's all.'

Jackie peered out of the passenger window, knowing that a few miles beyond the night-shrouded landscape were the even darker depths of the Bristol Channel. 'Maybe it's come in off the coast,' she said.

Joe made a non-committal sound. It was no kind of explanation, and they both knew it.

'Oh well,' he said, 'it *is* only fog, I s'pose. What's the worst that can happen?'

Without waiting for a reply, he pressed gently down on the accelerator and the car rumbled forward.

Entering the fog was like having a thick grey blanket thrown over them. Jackie tensed, clenching her fists, holding her breath. The light from the headlamps bounced back, as if from a mirror, dazzling them. Instinctively, Joe braked.

'I'm not happy about this,' he said.

'Just keep going,' said Jackie. 'It's a freak fog bank, that's all. Cold and warm air colliding or something. Just take it slowly and we'll be through it in a minute.'

Joe nodded, and for the next few minutes the car crept forward at little more than twenty miles an hour. All the while, the fog rushed and swirled towards them like something furious and alive. Mesmerised and unnerved, Jackie forced herself to blink, told herself she couldn't *really* see shapes trying to form from the muscular grey vapour. Her brain was simply trying to make sense of the constantly shifting shapelessness of it. It was a natural human reaction – like seeing faces in clouds, or looking for patterns in the chaos of nature.

It wasn't only her sight that was affected, though. She fancied she could *smell* the fog, like thick, sour soup, and she was equally certain that it was playing havoc with her hearing, filling her ears like cotton wool, blurring the music into a mushy buzz, reducing the throaty growl of the engine to flat, bland static. She opened her mouth wide, trying to yawn, hoping her ears might pop. And then she *did* yawn, and was dismayed to find that it made no difference. She felt a stab of anxiety. Maybe the fog was toxic; maybe it was affecting them physically, like nerve gas or something. She wondered whether she should say something to Joe, but she was almost afraid to speak, in case she found out that she could no longer string two words together.

And then suddenly, without warning, they were through.

It happened in a blink. One second they were crawling forward through impenetrable greyness, and the next the road ahead was clear, and the moon fat and bright again, spilling its light onto the land.

Joe was so shocked that he stamped on the brake, stalling the car.

'What just happened?'

Jackie jerked forward, her seatbelt clamping across her chest. Then she twisted round, to look out through the back windscreen. Incredibly there was no sign of the fog behind them. Just the evenly spaced lights above the carriageway, dwindling into blackness.

'I dunno,' she said. She was relieved that the fog had gone, but scared too.

'Ten past eleven,' Joe said, glancing at the glowing green digits of the dashboard clock.

'What's that got to do with anything?' Jackie asked.

Joe grinned, but it was sickly, feeble. 'I wondered whether we'd... lost a chunk of time. It's what's supposed to happen when people get abducted by aliens.'

'Abducted by aliens?' Jackie scoffed, fear making her

angrier than she would ordinarily have been. 'Are you serious?'

'No,' said Joe, 'I suppose not. We haven't lost time, in any case.' He grinned again, trying to make light of it. 'Maybe we should check each other for puncture wounds, though.'

'Let's just get home,' Jackie said.

Joe nodded and started the car up again. Jackie was wide awake now. They set off, and had been travelling for a minute in tense silence when Joe said, 'This can't be right.'

'What is it now?' Jackie asked.

'Is it just me or have we already been on this bit of road? About ten minutes back?'

She shrugged. 'Dunno. It all looks the same to me. Anyway, I was asleep.'

'Yeah, look,' he said, pointing, 'there's the sign for Bonvilston. This is just… this doesn't make sense.'

'Maybe there're two signs,' said Jackie.

Joe shook his head. 'No, that's definitely the one we passed ten minutes ago.'

'Well, it can't have been, can it?' The impossibility of the situation was making Jackie snappish again. She swallowed, trying to control her fear. 'You must have just… taken a wrong turn or something.'

'I've been driving in a straight line,' Joe said.

'It's the fog,' said Jackie. 'You must have driven up a slip road without realising it. Looped round in a circle. It's easily done.'

'Yeah, you're probably right,' said Joe, but he sounded unconvinced.

He drove on, mouth set in a grim line, hands gripping the wheel so tightly that his knuckles stood out in sharp white points. For a few minutes neither of them spoke. Both stared at the road ahead.

Then Jackie's eyes widened. 'Oh God,' she breathed.

The fog was back, same as before, a thick, solid wall of it, directly in front of them.

There was something intimidating about it. Something sinister and challenging. But when he spoke, Joe's voice was carefully upbeat, almost jaunty.

'Well, I suppose this supports your theory that we've come in a circle. We'll just have to be more careful this time.'

Jackie nodded, but said nothing. She felt the muscles in her arms and stomach tightening, instinctively pressed herself back into her seat as the fog enshrouded them again. She'd always hated roller-coasters, always hated that moment when the car clanked its way to the top of the incline and was inching forward in readiness for the downward plunge.

She felt like that now. That awful anticipation. That sense of being out of control and unable to do a thing about it.

Stupid, she told herself. *What is there to be scared—*

Without warning, a figure loomed out of the fog.

She only caught a glimpse of it before Joe was yelling, and yanking on the wheel, and the car was slewing

13

sideways. But in that split second she got the impression of someone tall and ragged and oddly lopsided; someone standing directly in the path of the car, head tilted to one side as if it was too heavy for the spindly neck that was supporting it. She saw no other details. The figure was nothing but a charcoal-grey silhouette on a pearly-grey background.

And then the car hit the figure side-on with a sickeningly loud bang, and the figure flew backwards, as though snatched away by some vast predator. Suddenly the car was spinning madly, and the tyres were screeching, and Jackie was being thrown about as if she weighed nothing.

Even as pain exploded in her shoulder and knee as she whacked them on the seat and door, a sharp, almost searing memory came to her of being seven years old and clinging to the safety bar of the waltzer in the fairground and wishing it would stop. And then, hot on the heels of that, she thought with an almost lucid calmness: *This is going to be the biggest impact I've ever known. I wonder if I'll die.*

Then suddenly there was silence, and she was lying at a strange angle across her seat, pressed back by the air bag. There was a smell in the air, fumes and hot metal, and she could taste blood in her mouth, and when she tried to move her leg a hot, jagged corkscrew of pain leaped from her shinbone to her hip, making her cry out.

Joe spoke. She couldn't see him, but she heard his voice, cracked and shaky. 'Jacks, are you OK?'

She opened her mouth to answer and it was full of blood. She spat it out.

'Hurt my leg,' she said.

She heard Joe shift beside her, then grunt softly in pain. 'I need to call for help,' he said, 'but I can't get a signal. I think it's this bloody fog.'

There was a screech of metal. Jackie couldn't think what it was at first, and then realised it must be the sound of the buckled driver's door being pushed open.

'What are you doing?' she said, fighting down panic.

'I need to get help,' he said again. 'I'm going to walk back along the road a bit, see if I can get a signal.'

'Don't leave me, Joe,' Jackie said.

'It'll only be for a few minutes. I need to call for an ambulance. And I need to find out what happened to that bloke we hit.'

'Don't leave me,' she said again.

'I'm not going to leave you,' he said. 'I'll be back in a few minutes, Jacks. Promise. Just… just try and relax, all right?'

She heard a creak of metal as he shifted his weight. A hiss of pain. Then the sound of his footsteps as he hobbled away, into the fog. His footsteps grew fainter, and then suddenly she couldn't hear them any more. She felt a sudden surge of loneliness, which threatened to escalate into outright panic. She breathed deeply, in and out, fighting to bring it under control. She told herself that everything would be fine, that Joe would get help, and that soon they would be in the hospital or at home, a bit bruised and battered, maybe, but wrapped up snug and warm in front of the telly, sipping nice hot cups of tea.

Because of the air bag she couldn't see much. Just a portion of the shattered passenger window and the swirling grey fog beyond. Curls of vapour were drifting in through the window, acrid and cold.

She was just beginning to wonder how much longer Joe was going to be when a terrible, ratcheting scream came tearing out of the fog.

It was an awful sound, barely human, and yet Jackie knew that it had come from her husband's throat. Gripped by freezing terror, she started to shake and cry. She tried to move, and her spine erupted with white-hot pain, so intense that she almost blacked out.

Then another scream tore into the echoes of the last, a high bubbling wail of pure agony. Now Jackie felt alternately hot and cold as sheer sickening panic surged through her. Terrified and helpless, she told herself that this couldn't be happening, it couldn't, it *couldn't*…

She tried to call her husband's name, to scream for help, but she couldn't make a sound.

Not even when she heard the slow, dragging footsteps coming towards the car.

Not even when a hand that was more bone than flesh reached in through the window.

ONE

'Right then, boys, who's up for a little jaunt round the Bay?'

It was Steffan who'd spoken. Toby looked at him, then glanced at the flushed faces around the glass-laden table. Not for the first time he found himself wondering whether a single one of his new friends – if that was really what they were – felt as dislocated and as... well, *homesick* as he did.

Like every other first-year, Toby had been at Cardiff University for about four weeks now. Four weeks of partying and drinking and meeting new people. Yet, despite it all, he *still* found himself trying to shake off the notion that he was an outsider, that he didn't fit in. Everyone else seemed to have cemented themselves quickly and easily into student life, so why hadn't he?

Though he would never have admitted it to anyone, he badly missed his mum and dad, and his mates, and all the familiar things and places back in Leicester. He missed his girlfriend Lauren, too, even though they'd decided to cool it a bit now that they were going off to different universities. God, he even missed his annoying little sister, Jess, and her obsession with MSN.

What's wrong with me? he thought. *Why can't I just enjoy myself? Why can't I just let myself go?*

Maybe it was the people. Maybe he'd fallen in with the wrong crowd. Sports Management attracted all sorts, but because of his room-mate, Curtis, he'd found himself stuck with the hard-drinking rugger-buggers. Toby had never thought of himself as a party pooper, but he just didn't see the point of getting blotto every night. It wasn't even as if drinking with this lot helped him loosen up; in fact, the more raucous and obnoxious his new friends became, the more he found himself retreating into his shell.

'What do you mean by a jaunt?' Curtis asked now. He was a Londoner, and wore his hair in short, beaded dreadlocks. He was tall and worked out a lot. He wore white skinny-fit T-shirts to emphasise his rippling muscles. The guys sometimes called him Audley because he looked like Audley Harrison, the boxer.

Steffan grinned, stood up and delved in his pockets. He was big and solid too, though not as toned as Curtis. He was from Newport, and because of his local knowledge he'd pretty much appointed himself leader of the group.

Nobody else seemed to mind, but Toby wasn't keen on Steffan. He found him arrogant and sarcastic and, despite his own homesickness, he couldn't help finding it a bit pathetic that the guy had chosen a university only a mile or two up the road from where his parents lived.

Steffan held up both hands. In one was a set of keys, in the other what looked like a black credit card.

'What's that?' asked Greg. He was a thick-necked Scouser, and he was so drunk that he could hardly keep his eyes open.

'These are the keys to my uncle's yacht,' Steffan said, jangling them, 'and this is the security fob that'll get us into Penarth Marina, where he keeps it.'

'Your uncle's got a *yacht*?' said Curtis in disbelief.

'Twelve-metre cruiser,' said Steffan smugly.

Stan, who was tall and rangy and had had football trials with QPR and his local team, Southport, shook his head, lank hair flapping like rat's tails across his face. 'How the other half lives.'

'What's he do then, this uncle of yours?' asked Curtis.

'He's a butcher,' said Steffan.

'Get lost!'

'Not a word of a lie. Got a meat-processing plant up in Merthyr, hasn't he? Makes a fortune from pies and sausages and that.'

'Does he know you've got the keys to his yacht?' asked Toby.

Steffan sneered. 'What do *you* think?' Then he shrugged. 'Not that he'd be bothered, mind. Long as we don't wreck it, he'll think it's a laugh, us taking it out for a midnight jaunt. He was a bit of a lad himself, in his day. Still is, I reckon.' He jangled the keys again. 'So what's it to be, boys? Who's up for it?'

Curtis glanced briefly round at the group, then nodded. 'Yeah, I'm in. Like you say, it'll be a laugh.'

'Me too,' said Stan. 'I ain't never been on a yacht before.'

'Greg?' said Steffan.

Greg raised a hand and waved it drunkenly. 'Yeah, whatever.'

Before anyone could ask him, Toby pushed his chair back. 'I think I'll give it a miss, guys, if you don't mind. I'm really tired and—'

Immediately there was a storm of protest.

If it had been good-natured banter, Toby might not have minded. But their comments were nasty, bullish, scathing. Steffan in particular made it clear that he thought Toby was not only snubbing them, but voicing his disapproval at the same time.

'Think you're better than us, you do,' he said.

'No, I don't,' said Toby.

'Yeah, you do. You think we're a load of idiots, just cos we like to have a laugh.'

'I didn't say that.'

'You didn't need to. You're like an old woman, all pursed lips and hoity-toity.'

Before Toby could respond, Stan said, 'I reckon he's just scared cos he thinks he'll get in trouble.'

Then they were all making chicken noises and flapping their arms like wings, and in the end Toby found himself tagging along just to save face. He trailed miserably in their wake as they crossed the Cardiff Bay Barrage to Penarth. He watched them shoving and jostling each other, giggling like kids on a school outing, and he felt more like a pariah than ever, even though it was they who'd insisted he come along.

He half-hoped they'd get some trouble at Penarth Quay, half-hoped the security fob would not be enough to grant them access to the Marina. But Steffan simply swiped the card, tapped in his uncle's security pin and they were through. The night-shift guy manning the Marina Office even waved to them as they passed by.

'Here it is, boys,' Steffan said a couple of minutes later. 'What do you think?'

As one, they goggled in drunken disbelief at the craft bobbing sedately on the water before them. The yacht was elegant and immaculately maintained. Constructed of gleaming white fibreglass, it had a single mast, plenty of deck space and a sizeable central cabin area. Even Toby couldn't help but be impressed, though the prospect of his drunken companions taking such a beautiful – and no doubt hideously expensive – vessel out on the water filled him with dread.

'This is so *sweet*, man,' exclaimed Curtis, laughing and clapping his hands.

'Bleedin' amazing,' nodded Stan, awestruck.

'Do you know how to drive it?' Toby asked nervously,

and again Steffan shot him a look so scathing that Toby decided that, starting tomorrow, he would find himself a new set of friends.

'Course I do. Nothing to it, is there. I mean, it's not as if we're going to encounter much *traffic*.'

The boys all sniggered at Toby's expense. Steffan leaped from the jetty to the deck, staggering a little.

'Well, come on then, gents. Climb aboard.'

One by one they stepped across the divide between jetty and deck. Greg, the drunkest of them, took a few tottering steps sideways and fell over. Toby laughed along with everyone else, but anxiety still gnawed away inside him. Steffan unlocked the door that led down to the living quarters.

'There's beers in the fridge, a bog at the far end, and there's even a bed for everyone, if you fancy a little lie down.'

Curtis descended the steps into the saloon, shaking his head in gleeful wonder. 'Man, I do not believe this,' he muttered. 'This is the *height* of luxury.'

'Only one rule,' Steffan said as Stan and Greg followed Curtis below decks. 'No throwing up down there. If you want to puke you do it over the side.'

Toby hesitated a moment, contemplating whether to join his friends. Then he turned away and walked over to lean on the metal guard rail which edged the perimeter of the deck, deciding that he couldn't stand another minute of their drunken banter. He stood on the seaward side, looking out over the black water, the chill winter wind ruffling his hair. He wondered what Lauren was doing now. She was at Durham University, and the last time he'd spoken to her, almost two weeks ago, she'd told him she was having a brilliant time.

'Feeling a bit dicky, are we?'

Steffan asked the question as though it was a failing. Toby half-turned to face him.

'No, just fancied some fresh air,' he said.

Steffan snorted, and headed towards the small wheelhouse, which contained the engine controls and navigational equipment. Toby sighed and turned back to gaze over the black water. Blades of reflected moonlight flashed and sparkled on the crests of the swells; tiny waves lapped against the hull. From the saloon floated snatches of throaty, ragged laughter. With a low rumble the engine started up, and then the yacht was moving, sliding out from its berth, heading into the Bay, like a vast and elegant marine creature released from captivity.

It cut through the water with barely a ripple, and within a few minutes they had left the lights of Cardiff Bay behind. Gradually Toby started to relax. It seemed as though Steffan knew how to handle the craft after all. Maybe this *wasn't* going to be the disaster he'd envisaged.

He breathed in the sharp, salty air and looked up at the moon. He wondered whether any of the guys below decks were talking about him, asking where he was. It still felt weird leaving home, cutting the apron strings. Ridiculous though it seemed, it hadn't sunk in that that was what he'd done until Mum and Dad had said goodbye after getting him settled into the poky room he shared with Curtis in one of the university's halls of residence. Oh, he would go home for Christmas, and even the odd weekend, but as far as living permanently with his parents was concerned, that part of his life was now over. He supposed when he graduated he'd find a job and get his own place somewhere. He'd been looking forward to his independence for a long time, had thought how great it would be to be answerable to nobody but himself – but he had to admit that the sudden reality of it had come as a bit of a shock.

Toby was so preoccupied with his own thoughts that he didn't notice the bank of fog until they were almost upon it. He glanced up, then stepped back from the rail in sudden shock. For a moment he'd thought they were about to hit something solid, a grey concrete wall stretching across the ocean. Certainly the fog seemed as straight and unbroken as a wall. It was weird the way it seemed to just sit on the surface of the sea like a barrier or something.

If Steffan in the wheelhouse had noticed the fog, he didn't seem perturbed by it. The yacht surged forward without faltering, and moments later the fog had swallowed them up.

Toby shuddered. There was an acrid smell, like sour milk or bad breath, and the fog itself had an almost oily texture to it. Tendrils coiled around him like the ghosts of eels. He remembered an old movie about a guy in a boat who starts to shrink after passing through a weird

24

kind of mist out at sea. Stupid, of course, but it made Toby hope that he wasn't inhaling anything poisonous.

He couldn't see more than a few metres in any direction. He hoped Steffan had sonar or radar or something up there in the wheelhouse. If some other vessel loomed out of the fog now, they wouldn't see it until it was too late. Toby listened, but heard nothing except an eerie silence. Rather than feeling relieved, however, he was suddenly struck by the awful notion that he was alone on the yacht, that Steffan and the others had gone, spirited away by something lurking out there in the dark depths of the ocean. He half-turned, intending to make his way to the wheelhouse, so desperate for human company that he was even prepared to put up with Steffan's contemptuous remarks. And then, as abruptly as it had appeared, the fog was gone.

Toby swayed, momentarily disorientated. What the hell was going on? A second ago he hadn't been able to see more than a metre or so in front of him, yet now the sky was clear again, the glittering stars diamond-sharp, the unveiled moon edging the curves and contours of the deck in hard white light.

He consoled himself with the thought that maybe this was normal; that maybe it was some common seafaring phenomenon; that maybe, as a sailor, you'd be used to this kind of thing happening all the time. Perhaps the best thing was simply to shrug it off, accept it as one of countless strange quirks in a world that was full of weirdness. He turned to settle himself once more against

25

the guard rail when he heard pounding footsteps behind him. Looking round he saw Steffan approaching across the deck, a scowl on his face.

'What the hell's going on?' the Welshman demanded.

For a moment Toby thought he was being accused of something, and then he realised that it was a rhetorical question. Steffan all but threw himself against the guard rail, glaring at the sea as though issuing it a challenge.

Hesitantly Toby asked, 'How do you mean?'

Steffan glanced at him. 'Bloody navigation's gone haywire, hasn't it?' He swung round, then did an almost classic double take. 'This is mad,' he muttered.

Toby followed his gaze. At first he wasn't sure what he was seeing, and then all at once it struck him.

The lights of Cardiff Bay, although still some distance away, were bright enough not only to delineate the shape of the shoreline, but to highlight details of many of the buildings clustered at the water's edge. The effect was undeniably attractive – the pattern of lights coalescing to bathe the land in a welcoming glow – and yet this particular view should not have been visible at all. They had left the lights of Cardiff Bay behind them some time ago. Toby himself had watched them dwindle and wink out, until all that was left was a vague orange haze, like a distant fire on the horizon.

'What do you think's happened?' he asked.

'I don't know, do I?' snapped Steffan. Then his face changed from anger to an almost boyish confusion. 'It's impossible, that's what it is.'

'We must have turned round in the fog,' said Toby.

'We haven't.'

'But we *must* have.'

Steffan's lips curled to deliver some harsh rejoinder, but at that moment Curtis, Stan and a dazed-looking Greg came pounding up the steps from below.

'What's that noise, man?' Curtis demanded.

Steffan turned irritably. '*What* noise?'

'I think we've hit something,' Stan said.

Steffan's face flushed, the heat rising up from the collar of his pale blue polo shirt, suffusing his ears and cheeks. 'Course we haven't,' he barked. 'We're out in the middle of the Bay, you daft sod.'

'Well, *something* was scraping against the bottom of the boat,' said Curtis.

'We all heard it,' added Stan.

'Could've been a shipwreck or something,' Curtis suggested.

'A shipwreck?' Steffan's voice was a strangled croak. 'What do you think this is? Pirates of the bloody Caribbean?'

Curtis's brow furrowed, and he was about to respond when they heard a deep, steady pounding beneath their feet, followed by a more irregular series of thuds and bangs. They all looked at each other. Steffan's face was puce now, his eyes all but popping out of his head.

'What the hell was that?' said Toby quietly.

Stan had wandered across to the side of the boat and was peering over the guard rail. 'Er... boys,' he said.

'What now?' barked Steffan.

'There's, er, something in the water.'

They all crowded up to the guard rail to look. Toby saw a dozen or more dark, spherical objects bobbing on the gentle black swells, which rose and fell around the yacht.

'What are they?' asked Curtis. 'Seals?'

'Maybe they're lifebuoys,' said Stan.

Toby caught a flash of movement to his left. He looked around just in time to see a grey hand reach up over the side of the deck and curl around the lowest rung of the guard rail.

He stepped back on to Greg's toe, his mouth dropping open. Stan had seen the hand now too. He let out an incoherent croak and pointed.

Toby had time to observe that the hand was wrinkled and pitted, that strips of flesh were hanging off it like rags.

Then he saw the hand tighten and haul the rest of the body into view, and suddenly it felt as though the air had been wrenched from his lungs.

The creature must once have been human, but now its face was a hollow ruin. Wriggling white eels poured from its empty eye sockets and gaping mouth, spattering on the deck in writhing clumps. The creature's clothes were nothing but colourless tatters, its ribs showing between the rents in its saturated grey flesh. It turned its head towards them, and Toby had the feeling that it could see – or at least sense – them, despite the fact that it had no eyes.

The boys clustered together instinctively, like sheep menaced by a wolf. Toby heard Stan muttering 'shit' over and over; he heard someone whimpering like a child – he thought it might be Steffan. He himself was silent, his mind numb with disbelief; he actually wondered whether he might be dreaming. He looked to his left, and saw another corpse hauling itself over the side of the boat. It was a woman this time, her face purple and bloated, her floral-patterned dress covered in slime. Then there was a noise behind them, and a child scrambled crab-like onto the deck, dripping weed tangled in its hair, the wound in its throat so severe that Toby could see its spinal column through it. Within moments the yacht was overrun, the dead swarming up out of the water from all directions.

With nowhere to run, Toby squeezed his eyes tightly shut and thought of Lauren.

TWO

Gwen was awake in an instant, her hand reaching for her gun. But her gun wasn't there; of course it wasn't. She was at home in bed, curled beneath the duvet in her jim-jams, Rhys snoring quietly beside her.

She sat up, pushing a curtain of glossy black hair out of her face. She imagined she could still hear the scream that had woken her, echoing in the silence. Could it have been a dream? It was possible. She'd had plenty of nightmares since Owen and Tosh had died on that awful day. She knew she'd been a bit clingy with Rhys since then, but he'd been brilliant. She looked down at him now, one hand tucked under his head, mouth slightly open, and she smiled. She reached out to gently stroke his hair... and heard the clanging clatter of a dustbin lid from the back alley.

She was out of bed, across the narrow landing and wrestling with the stiff catch of the bathroom window before the edge of the duvet had even settled into place behind her. Finally winning her battle with the catch, she shoved the window open and stuck her head out.

She couldn't see much. The angles were all wrong. Just a jutting length of wall, stretching down to a sliver of ground, and the edge of a dustbin, viewed from above, peeking around the corner. All of it was soaked in the orange light of an overhead lamp, and gleamed grittily in the drizzle that Gwen could feel speckling the back of her exposed neck.

Ducking back inside, she tugged the window shut, shivering at the chill.

'What's going on?' said a voice behind her.

She spun, startled. Rhys was standing there in T-shirt and boxers, face rumpled from sleep, hair sticking up every which way.

'Rhys!' Gwen gasped and slapped him lightly on the chest. 'Don't do that to me. I nearly had a heart attack.'

He grinned boyishly. 'Oh, that's charming, that is. Frightened of me after all the horrible things you've seen.' He nodded at the now-closed window. 'What you doing anyway?'

'I heard something,' she said.

'One of those Weevil things, was it?'

'I heard a scream. *Thought* I heard a scream. It woke me up. Then I heard a clatter, like a dustbin lid falling off.'

'Want me to go have a look?'

She couldn't help smiling. 'Don't be daft. If anyone's going to go, it should be me.'

Rhys looked offended. 'Hey, you might be a rough, tough defender of the planet at work, *Mrs Williams*, but let a bloke have a bit of pride in his own home.'

Gwen chuckled and kissed him on the forehead. 'Fine. We'll go together.'

Two minutes later they had dragged on clothes and boots and were hurrying down the stairs of the apartment block. Ignoring the front door, they headed towards the heavily bolted door at the back of the building, which led out into the narrow alleyway threading between their street and the one parallel. Gwen reached the door as Rhys was still thumping down the last flight of stairs, and began drawing back the thick bolts.

'Let me go first,' Rhys panted.

Gwen used one hand to twist the catch on the door and the other to produce her Torchwood-issue semi-automatic from inside her leather jacket.

'I'm the one with the gun,' she replied, raising her eyebrows.

Rhys pulled a face. 'Come on, love, bit of an overreaction, don't you think? Not every disturbance in Cardiff is caused by psychotic aliens, you know. It's more likely to be Betty Prudom's cat.'

'I know, but still… better safe than sorry,' Gwen said and slipped outside.

By the time Rhys had followed her into the chill drizzle of the night, Gwen was already stalking down the alley, black and silent, looking not unlike a cat herself. Her shadow stretching out long and thin before her, she moved towards the brick extension jutting from the rear of the building, which narrowed the alley still further and hid the line of dustbins from view.

Rhys hurried towards her, footsteps crackling on the wet ground. She turned and placed a finger to her lips. He rolled his eyes.

'Listen,' she whispered.

He listened. Something was moving in the alley, shuffling around near the bins. Something that sounded bigger than a cat.

Left hand cupped around her right, in which she held her gun, Gwen crept forward. She reached the wall, flattened her back against it, sidled up to the edge and peered around the corner.

She went very still. Rhys was beside her now, feeling like a bit of a spare part.

'Well?' he hissed. 'What can you see?'

Her head jerked round to look at him, hair swishing across her face. Her eyes were wide, face taut with disbelief.

'What is it, Gwen? Talk to me,' he said.

Suddenly she was a blur of movement. Instead of replying, she swung out into the alley, body poised and balanced, arms extended, gun pointing at whatever was moving about by the bins.

'Get up slowly,' she barked. 'Keep your hands where I can see them.'

For a split second Rhys wondered whether he ought to stay where he was, out of sight. Then he thought, *Sod that*, and moved across to stand beside his wife.

He had a clear view of the alley now, all the way to the sagging chain-link fence at the far end. To their immediate right, snug against the back of the house, was a line of metal dustbins, one per flat, each with a big white number painted on its lid.

Rhys barely registered any of this. He was too busy goggling at the figure squatting on the ground no more than five metres away. He shuddered as a wave of revulsion and cold, prickling fear swept through him.

The man – a tramp, judging by the rags he was wearing – was eating a cat. Rhys thought it might be the old ginger tom which belonged to Betty, their downstairs neighbour, but it was hard to be sure. The poor animal had been ripped apart and devoured, like a roast chicken at a medieval banquet. Most of its remains were lying on the ground at the man's feet, a mangled mass of fur and gore. Even now, as if oblivious to their presence, the man was gnawing on one of the animal's detached limbs, his chin and clothes smeared liberally in blood and guts.

'Oh, Christ,' Rhys muttered, 'that's disgusting.'

Gwen glanced at him, then turned back to the man. 'I told *you* to *stand up!*' she shouted.

The man paused, and then he cocked his head in a strangely animalistic way, as if Gwen's voice was very faint and it was taking him a long time to register her words.

And then his head snapped up with a sudden, horrible jerk, and they saw his face properly for the first time.

'Oh God,' Rhys murmured.

The man had no nose. Just a hole where his nose should have been. And his eyes were milky white. And his skin, dry and brown like old leaves, was stretched so tightly across the jutting bones of his skull that his mouth seemed lipless, exposing his black gums and blocky, meat-clogged teeth. As the man lurched upright, Rhys noticed other things about him too. He noticed that one of the man's fingers was missing at the second knuckle, and that the bone was sticking out like a splintered stick; he noticed that the man's feet were bare, and that the skin covering them had split in places, to reveal the sinews and tendons beneath.

And he noticed the smell. The awful, stomach-churning stench of something dead.

The man let out a sound from his ravaged throat, a horrible animal sound that was somewhere between a groan and a snarl. Then he raised his gore-gloved hands and lurched towards them.

'*Get back!*' Gwen screamed at him. '*Get back, or God help me, I'll shoot you!*'

The man didn't even falter. He came at them, his face twisting into an expression of malice that was somehow mindless, utterly devoid of conscious thought.

Gwen shot him. The bullet blasted into his shoulder, leaving a sizeable hole, chunks of flesh and bone flying in all directions.

The man spun and fell, knocked back by the impact. Lowering her gun slightly, but still wary, Gwen took a step towards him.

The man scrambled to his feet and lurched towards them again. Gwen stepped back, almost slipping. Rhys grabbed her arm.

'Come on, love. You're not going to stop him. Let's just run.'

Gwen looked shaken and bewildered. She nodded, and the two of them ran back to the door leading into the apartment block. However, the door was on a spring and had clicked shut behind them. Mouth dry, Rhys delved into his jeans pocket with a trembling hand. It was a tight fit and the key ring was tangled up with all sorts of other stuff – loose change, a crumpled tissue, receipts from work.

'Come *on*, Rhys,' Gwen said. 'It's right behind us.'

'I'm trying,' he said.

'Well, try a bit harder.'

Rhys could hear the shuffling approach of the thing coming up behind them. Could hear its awful snarling groan. Snarling himself, he grabbed the key ring and wrenched. Money and paper flew out of his pocket, but he didn't care. With fingers that felt fat and clumsy, he found the right key and shoved it into the lock. The key turned, the door opened, and they tumbled into the building.

Gwen slammed the door shut and slid the bolts home, while Rhys, his legs suddenly very shaky, sank to the floor. He was sweating and gasping, as though he had just run the 400 metres. He clenched his fists to stop his hands from shaking.

Gwen stepped back from the door as a heavy weight slammed against it from the other side. The thing growled in apparent frustration, and continued to slam against the door, as though unable to understand why it couldn't get at them.

Rhys looked up at Gwen, who was blinking and taking deep breaths.

'I'm not imagining it, am I?' he said. 'That bloke *was* dead, wasn't he?'

Gwen rolled her eyes, shrugged and snorted out a laugh that had no humour in it whatsoever. Then she took her mobile out of her pocket.

'I'm calling Jack,' she said.

THREE

'You ready yet, Kirst?' called Sophie, pushing open the door of the ladies'.

'Two more minutes,' Kirsty shouted back. 'Just putting my face on.'

It had been a busy night in *El Puerto*, the fish and meat restaurant located in the Old Custom House, just across the road from Penarth Marina. But then *every* night in *El Puerto* was busy. The place was an incessant buzz of energy and conviviality and, from the beginning to the end of their shift, Sophie Gould and her best friend Kirsty Lane were constantly on the move, scurrying between tables, taking orders, pouring wine and champagne, and delivering plates of red snapper, steaming lobster and sea bass to hungry punters. It was hard work, but they loved it, and the tips alone were almost enough to pay for a decent night out.

As Kirsty finally emerged from the loo, snapping shut her sequinned shoulder bag, Terry, the deputy manager, appeared from behind the display counter, wiping his hands on a tea towel.

'You two must really love this place,' he said.

'Been getting ready, haven't we?' said Kirsty.

'We're going clubbing,' Sophie added.

'Blimey, you've got some stamina, I'll say that for you.'

Kirsty winked at him. 'A lot more than you could handle, mate.'

She was tiny and raven-haired, with big brown eyes, and it was obvious to Sophie that Terry fancied her rotten. As the deputy manager blushed through a grin, Sophie said, 'Come on, Kirst, let's be off. Save your flirting muscles for later.'

Saying goodnight to Terry, they tottered towards the door on their heels. They were almost there when he called after them. 'By the way, while you two were out back beautifying yourselves, you missed all the excitement.'

Kirsty glanced back at him. 'What excitement was that, then?'

'There's something going on down by the Marina, isn't there,' he told them. 'They've cordoned it all off. There's police, ambulances, the lot.'

Now Kirsty turned her big, shining eyes on her friend. She loved a bit of drama. 'Hey, come on, Soph, let's have a nosy.'

Sophie sighed. She'd much rather be downing a spritzer in a nice bar than standing out in the cold, but she knew there was no stopping Kirsty when she got a bee in her bonnet.

'Two minutes, tops,' she conceded. 'I'm not standing around all night.'

They went outside. It was not hard to identify the site of the incident. Quite a crowd had already gathered behind a sizeable barrier of fluorescent yellow tape. A standing metal sign read: POLICE RESTRICTED ZONE. Parked within the barrier were a pair of ambulances and four police cars, their blue lights flashing silently. Arc lamps had been set up down by the jetty and seemed to be trained on a yacht berthed beside a police patrol boat. Uniformed men milled everywhere.

Kirsty tapped a fellow rubbernecker on the shoulder. He was an elderly gent with a white moustache, wearing a navy blue blazer, white slacks and white shoes. Sophie was pretty sure she'd seen him earlier in the restaurant.

'What's going on, mister?' Kirsty asked.

The elderly man looked her up and down before answering. When he opened his mouth to speak, Sophie noticed with distaste that his teeth were very yellow.

'I've no idea,' he said waspishly. 'All I know is that I'm unable to get access to my boat. It's damned inconvenient.'

A younger, thicker-set man turned round. His accent identified him as a local. 'They reckon there's been a murder.'

'That's what the police have said, is it?' Sophie asked.

'Well… not as such,' the man admitted. 'Not to me, anyway. But that's what everyone reckons.'

Sophie touched her friend on the arm. 'Aw, c'mon, Kirst, let's go. Whatever's happening, we'll read about it in the paper tomorrow.'

Kirsty had the expression of a little kid being dragged away from a funfair. 'Just a couple more minutes,' she pleaded.

'What's the point? We won't find out anything. It's not like they're going to make an announce—'

The end of her sentence was cut off by the roar of a powerful engine and the screech of brakes from behind them. She turned to see a shiny black SUV with smoked windows, lines of flickering blue lights edging the windscreen. The front doors opened and two men jumped out. One was a handsome, chisel-jawed man who looked to be somewhere in his late thirties. With his army greatcoat, navy blue shirt, braces, chinos and boots, he reminded Sophie of an old-fashioned hero from a boy's adventure comic. His companion was younger, grim-faced but kind of sweet-looking. He wore an immaculate charcoal-grey suit, a white shirt and a pink-and-purple striped silk tie, and was fiddling with his cufflinks as he emerged from the SUV. Sophie noticed that both men had fancy little Bluetooth devices attached to their ears, and wondered if they were 'spooks', like off the telly.

'Make way, ladies and gentlemen. No photographs please,' the older man called in an American accent, cutting through the crowd. There was a wide and rather charming smile on his face and, whilst his voice was jocular, Sophie sensed that there was steel beneath his words.

Beside her, Kirsty was staring at the new arrivals. 'Lush,' she breathed.

They watched the two guys reach the police cordon and have a quick conversation with the officer on duty. They were quickly allowed through and hurried towards the yacht, the coat of the older man flowing behind him like a superhero's cape.

'I wonder who they are,' said Sophie.

'Dunno,' Kirsty replied dreamily, 'but they can enter my restricted zone any day.'

'OK, boys and girls,' Jack said heartily, 'what have you got for us?'

Ianto saw Detective Sergeant Swanson raise her eyebrows. She was a tall, slim, beautiful black woman in an immaculately tailored grey suit. The beads in her braided hair clicked gently together whenever she moved her head. She and Torchwood – and she and Jack in particular – had a love/hate relationship, which Jack seemed to revel in. In fact, Jack had once remarked that you could cook eggs on the heat of the sexual tension between him and the statuesque policewoman. Ianto hadn't been sure whether Jack was joking, and therefore couldn't now work out whether he ought to be jealous or not.

'Well, well, look what the cat's dragged in,' Swanson said.

She was standing with a colleague, a shorter, pudgy man in a wrinkled blue suit, who sniggered.

'Which must make *you* the cat,' Jack said, and raised his eyebrows. 'You got the costume to go with that?'

Swanson looked outraged. 'You don't honestly think *I* called you, do you, Jack? Why the hell would *I* want Torchwood stomping all over *my* investigation?'

'Maybe you just can't resist my baby blue eyes,' Jack said.

'Oh, *please*,' Swanson replied.

'It was a Detective Inspector Myers who called us,' Ianto said a little stiffly.

Swanson pulled a face. 'That figures.'

'He said there were some unusual aspects to the case. In fact, his actual words were, "This one's weirder than a three-headed monkey."'

Jack looked unimpressed. 'I dated a three-headed monkey once. What a summer *that* was!'

'Is this just one big joke to you, Jack?' Swanson said. 'Because it isn't to me. Five boys have died here tonight.'

The smile slipped from Jack's face. All at once he was sombre, business-like. 'What happened?'

'Why don't you see for yourselves?' Swanson said. There was a challenge in her voice as she added, 'I hope you've got strong stomachs.'

Jack flashed her a look, and he and Ianto hurried along the jetty towards the illuminated yacht. A team of forensics examiners, ghostly in their white all-in-ones, were moving around the deck, photographing evidence and making notes. Even from some distance away, Ianto saw that the gleaming fibreglass structure of the central cabin area was splashed liberally with blood. As he and Jack approached the boat, one of the officers spotted them and hurried over.

'Can I help you?'

'Captain Jack Harkness – Torchwood,' Jack said importantly.

'Ianto Jones,' said Ianto.

'Oh, so *you're* the famous Torchwood, are you?' said the officer, trying to look blasé. 'I'm Guy Baker, SOCO on this investigation. I take it you know the rules?'

'Rules are for—' Jack began, but Ianto jumped in.

'Don't touch anything. Don't contaminate the crime scene,' he recited.

'That's it.' Baker wafted a hand, as though inviting them aboard. 'Aside from that, have fun.'

Jack and Ianto stepped across the divide between jetty and deck, Ianto trying to keep his expression neutral as he looked around. There were pools and splashes of blood all over the deck, not to mention a copious amount of human remains. Most of the remains were unidentifiable – nothing but shreds and gobbets of mangled flesh and bone – but here and there were body parts that were patently, stomach-churningly human. Ianto saw a hand with two fingers missing, but part of the arm still attached; a section of gnawed ribcage; a long bone that might have been a femur; a head whose face was mercifully obscured by blood-matted hair.

Grim-faced, Jack asked Baker, 'So what are we looking at here? Animal attack?'

Baker shook his head. 'No. Believe it or not, the killers were human.'

Jack and Ianto glanced at each other. 'How many?' asked Jack.

'So far we've identified bite marks from thirteen different sets of teeth.'

'Unlucky for some,' Ianto murmured.

'And the victims were killed how?' Jack asked.

Baker spread his hands, as if he couldn't quite believe his own findings. 'As far as we can tell, they were simply… torn apart. Evidence suggests that the attackers used their bare hands to murder their victims and then cannibalised the bodies. Devoured them, in fact.'

Ianto placed a hand over his mouth and said nothing. He was thinking of cannibals up in the Brecon Beacons, not long after Gwen had joined Torchwood. The memory was not a happy one.

Jack was equally silent for a moment, and then he said, 'Detective Swanson said there were five victims?'

Baker nodded. 'We think they were all Cardiff University students. We found a couple of NUS cards among the debris.'

'What about the perpetrators?' Ianto asked.

'No sign. We think they must have pulled up in a boat alongside the yacht.'

'Won't there be a record of them in that case?' said Jack.

'We're looking into that now.'

'OK. Well, keep up the good work, Guy – and keep us informed. And now, if you don't mind, we'd like a little look round on our own.'

Baker did not exactly huff, but it was clear he did not appreciate being dismissed by Jack. As soon as he had moved away, Ianto took his PDA out of his pocket and turned it on.

'Anything?' Jack asked.

Ianto consulted the results scrolling across the display reader. 'There's residual Rift energy,' he said, 'but the percentage is almost low enough to be considered negligible.'

Jack looked thoughtful. 'So what do you think? That human beings did this?'

'Don't see why not. They were probably high on drugs. A cult, maybe.'

Jack gave him a look.

'What?' said Ianto, as if he was being accused of something.

'You know what I'm thinking, don't you?' Jack said.

Ianto shook his head. 'No, Jack. It's ridiculous. You *know* it's ridiculous.'

Almost smugly Jack said, 'On our way here we field a call from Gwen, who says that she and Rhys have been attacked by a walking corpse. And now here we are surrounded by evidence of an attack in which the perpetrators used their *bare hands* as murder weapons and then cannibalised their victims. What does that suggest to *you*, Ianto?'

Unhappily Ianto shook his head. 'It's crazy, Jack. It's horror-movie hokum. You know it is.'

'And *you* know what we're up against here, don't you?'

'No, I don't. Don't say it, Jack. Don't use the—'

'Zombies!' Jack exclaimed.

'— zed word,' Ianto concluded miserably.

FOUR

PC Andy Davidson took a left into Gabalfa Road. There was no need to scan the house numbers to pinpoint the source of the disturbance. An ambulance had already arrived, and was parked at the kerb, hazards flashing. Some people had spilled out of the house and were standing in the overgrown front garden, or on the pavement. Most looked drunk and confused, though one or two were arguing amongst themselves, gesticulating angrily at the house and each other.

'You all right?' Andy asked, glancing at Dawn Stratton, his new partner.

Dawn rolled her pale green eyes. 'I've already told you, Andy, you don't have to mollycoddle me.'

'Only asking,' Andy said, and switched off the engine. 'It's for my benefit as much as yours.'

'I'm fine,' she said firmly, and opened the door.

The call had come in five minutes earlier – a disturbance at a party in a student-occupied house. According to the caller, a gatecrasher had attacked and wounded a female partygoer.

Andy and Dawn strode across to the ambulance, Andy fending off comments from a couple of the more abrasive drunks. The back doors of the vehicle were standing open and a yellow-jacketed paramedic was inside, tending to a young girl.

'Hi,' Andy said, leaning in. He winced at the sight of the wound on the girl's arm. 'That looks nasty. Bitten, were you?'

The girl nodded. She was slightly built, pale and trembling with shock. The crescent of teeth-marks on her forearm was deep and still leaking blood.

'Who did this to you?' Andy asked gently.

The girl licked her lips. In a small voice she said, 'Dunno. Just some guy. He was like an animal. Think he was high on something.'

'And where's this guy now?' asked Dawn, standing at Andy's shoulder.

'In the cellar. Some of the other guys locked him in. He was a nutter. Going for everybody.'

'Don't worry, love, we'll sort him out,' Andy said. 'Any other injuries?' he asked the paramedic.

'Just minor stuff,' the paramedic replied. 'Cuts and scratches mainly. My colleague's inside, dealing with those.'

Andy thanked him, and then he and Dawn walked up the path and through the open door of the terraced house. The second paramedic was at the bottom of the stairs, crouched beside a girl who was perched on the third step, holding her blonde hair away from a pair of thin scratches on the side of her neck. The two police officers acknowledged the paramedic with a nod and stepped into a crowded room on their left. It was a typical student place – shabby decor; threadbare furniture; posters on the walls; cans, bottles and overflowing ashtrays cluttering every surface. The dimly lit room stank of cigarette smoke, and was so hot that the windows streamed with condensation. Music was blasting out of a sound system in the corner. Andy recognised it – he had the CD at home. Kings of Leon. *Only By The Night*.

'Can you turn that down a bit, please?' he asked a girl with dyed red hair and a nose stud, who was clutching a bottle of cider. The girl complied without a murmur, and Andy pointed at an open door in the far corner, which afforded enough of a glimpse of the room beyond to suggest that it led to a brightly lit kitchen. 'Cellar through here, is it?'

Heads nodded dutifully. As Andy and Dawn crossed to the door, the crowd parted before them.

The kitchen was narrow, and looked out on to a bricked-in backyard. Beside the greasy oven, cans and bottles bobbed in a plastic bath full of iced water. There were more bottles stacked on the work surfaces, and two black plastic dustbins full of empties stood by the back door. There were six guys in the kitchen, looking tense. One was swigging red wine out of a bottle; the rest were clutching cans of beer. Two were smoking roll-ups. A thin haze of blue-grey smoke hovered near the ceiling.

'Hello, fellers,' Andy said amiably. 'I gather you've got a bloke locked in your cellar?'

As if on cue, there was an irregular tattoo of thumps on the blue-painted door tucked away in an alcove at the back of the room. Accompanying the thumps was a low moan.

'Is he all right in there?' Dawn asked.

'He's a mentalist,' one of the guys muttered.

'Stinks an' all,' added another.

Andy crossed to the door and rested his forehead against the wood. 'Hello in there,' he said. 'This is the police. We're here to investigate an alleged assault. Could you tell me your name, please?'

There was a renewed barrage of thumps and moans from the other side of the door. Andy looked briefly at Dawn and raised his eyebrows, before trying again.

'I think you need to calm down, sir. Getting aggressive won't do anyone any good, least of all yourself. Now, can you please tell me your name?'

This time the thumps were accompanied by the sound of violent scratching. The moans became a series of guttural snarls.

Andy sighed and stepped back from the door. 'What can you tell me about this bloke?' he asked.

The six students all looked at each other. The one with

the wine bottle said, 'He just burst in. He was growling and, like, slashing at people. Then he grabbed Hayley's arm and bit it. She screamed like hell.'

The tallest and broadest of the boys said, 'Me and Martin jumped on him and got him on the floor. But he was totally crazed. It took six of us to get him in there.'

'You six?' asked Dawn.

They all nodded.

'So what's he like, this guy?' asked Andy. 'Describe him to me.'

'He looks rough,' said the gangly, bearded youth who had been identified as Martin. 'He's about… I dunno, thirty maybe. Not thin, but he looks like a junkie. White skin and weird eyes. And like Jace said, he stinks like he's been sleeping in a rubbish dump. His clothes are disgusting.' He pulled a face. 'We all had to wash our hands after touching him.'

Andy nodded. 'OK, well we'll take it from here. If you could clear the kitchen and close the door.'

The boys trooped out, evidently grateful to relinquish responsibility for the gatecrasher.

'You ready for this?' Andy said.

Dawn smiled thinly. 'Cuffs at the ready.'

Andy approached the door again. Taking a deep breath, he said, 'I'm going to open this door now, sir. I want you to come out quietly and keep your hands where we can see them. If you show any aggression towards either myself or my partner, we'll be forced to arrest you. Do you understand me?'

The only responses were further thumps and snarls.

Andy pulled a face at Dawn, who smiled back nervously, and then he reached out and slowly slid free the bolts at the top and bottom of the door. Equally slowly he twisted the key in the lock. Then he pulled the door open and stepped smartly back.

Without preamble the man lunged at him. Andy saw only a glazed stare and an oddly slack expression on a face so horribly pale it was almost blue, before hands were clawing at his face.

He reached up and grabbed the man's forearms. Stepping back, he used the man's forward momentum to twist him round and bear him to the ground.

The man landed on his stomach, hitting the floor with a thump as Andy twisted his arms behind his back. It should have been a standard arrest, but as Dawn was kneeling to slap handcuffs on the man's wrists, he suddenly surprised Andy by twisting from his grasp like an eel. Seemingly unaffected by having just had all the breath knocked out of him, he flipped around, reached out and grabbed Dawn's hand. She was so shocked that she dropped the handcuffs, which hit the linoleum floor with a metallic clatter. Before either she or Andy could respond, the man half sat up, dipped his head forward and sank his teeth into Dawn's hand.

She yelped in pain and instinctively punched the man in the side of the head with her other hand. It had no effect whatsoever. The man was like a dog, his teeth locked into Dawn's flesh, snarling as blood bubbled out of the wound.

Andy scrambled across the floor, getting behind the man and wrapping an arm around his neck. He grabbed the man's nose in his other hand and wrenched his head up and back, not caring if he broke the bastard's neck.

It did the trick. The man's jaw unlocked and Dawn wrenched her hand free with a cry of agony. Still the man snarled and writhed in Andy's grasp. He seemed impervious to pain, his lips curled back over bloodstained teeth, his jaw still working to bite any flesh that came within range. The lower half of his face was a mask of Dawn's blood; his white shirt was speckled and streaked with red.

Considering how wasted the man seemed, Andy was amazed at his tensile strength. He could only assume it was drug-fuelled. Certainly he had to use every ounce of his own strength to heave the man onto his front and wrench his arms behind his back. Dawn's hand was bleeding copiously, but she scooted forward to help, grabbing the handcuffs and securing them around the man's wrists.

Finally they had him restrained, though even now he bucked and twisted like a fish in a net. Andy stood up, sweating and panting. Dawn stood up too, but almost immediately staggered over to a chair and sat down again.

She took deep breaths, looking almost as pale as her attacker. Her injured hand hung between her knees, blood running down it, dripping onto the floor.

'We need to get that cleaned up,' Andy said.

Voice low and scared, Dawn replied, 'What if he's HIV positive? What if he's... infected me?'

There was a beat of silence. Then Andy said, 'We'll get the paramedics to check you out. Don't worry, I'm sure you'll be all right.'

She looked up at him, scowling. 'You don't *know* that,' she said.

Andy's face twitched into an expression somewhere between compassion and apology. 'No I don't. Sorry. But try not to worry, OK? Chances are, you'll be fine.'

She nodded, took another deep breath, and then stood up shakily. Andy helped her wash her hand at the sink and wrap it in a tea towel. Together they hauled the still-snarling, still-struggling man to his feet and then Andy frogmarched him towards the kitchen door.

'There's something really wrong with him,' she said.

'Tell me something I don't know,' replied Andy.

Dawn shook her head. 'No, I mean, really. Look at him. His skin's all marbled. His eyes are sunken and dead, like there's nothing there, like he's blind or something. I've seen corpses that look healthier than him. And he smells like death too.'

It was true. The man smelled like a week-old cadaver. Even when Andy had been grappling with him, he'd been uncomfortably aware of how the man's skin felt beneath his hands – damp and somehow greasy.

'Let's just get him down to the station,' he said. 'The doc can look at him there. Clear a way through, will you, Dawn? We don't want him biting anyone else.'

She nodded and opened the door into the crowded front room. 'Please move back,' she shouted, sweeping her uninjured hand left and right, as though parting curtains. Partygoers glanced at her and then stepped hurriedly aside, many clearly alarmed by the sight of their snarling, bloodstained captive.

They were almost at the door into the hallway when they heard shouts and screams from outside. Next moment, people were pouring into the house, stumbling and falling over one another in their haste.

'Hey! Hey!' Dawn shouted, as she was pushed and jostled. Instinctively, she reached out with her bandaged hand and grabbed the arm of a thin guy, who was running past. She winced at the pain, but maintained her grip. 'What's going on?'

The guy's wide-eyed alarm turned to momentary anger. Then he registered Dawn's uniform and said breathlessly, 'They appeared from nowhere. They're attacking people. Tearing them apart.'

'Who are?' asked Andy.

The guy's attention shifted to look over Dawn's shoulder. His gaze fixed on the slavering creature that Andy was holding in an arm lock, and his eyes widened.

'They're like him! They're *all* like him!'

Then he was gone, running towards the back of the house, overcome with panic.

Andy and Dawn exchanged a glance, and pushed their way through the now-dwindling inrush of people to the front door. They could still hear screams from outside. One series of raw, agonised shrieks chilled Andy to the core, before it was abruptly cut off. Shoving their captive before them, he and Dawn exited the house – and there they froze. The scene before them was one of such appalling carnage that for a moment they could do nothing but stare.

In the overgrown front garden, not five metres away from them, two men with the same dead-eyed, slack-jawed expressions as the arrested gatecrasher were delving into the gaping stomach of a young girl with their bare hands. The girl was still twitching, but clearly beyond help. The men, drenched in gore, were scooping out handfuls of her innards and eating them.

In the middle of the road, soaked in the pumpkin-orange light of the overhead street lamps, a young, dark-haired man was lying on his front, kicking and whimpering as a crowd of five people – three of them women – tore and slashed and gouged at his exposed back with their bare hands.

Yet another murderous crowd were clustered around the back of the still-open ambulance, bumping and blundering into one another as they tried to get at the vehicle's contents. Andy couldn't see what had become of the paramedic and the young girl with the bite on her arm, but he could see that the hands, faces and clothes of the majority of the attackers were stained with fresh blood.

It wasn't until a naked man reeled clumsily away from the back of the ambulance, however, chewing on a chunk of raw and bloody meat, that Andy realised exactly what he was witnessing. With a dreamy kind of horror, he saw that not only did the naked man have a gaping black hole in the left side of his face, but also that his chest and stomach, stretching from his groin to his collar bone, bore an ugly Y-shaped post mortem scar, stitched with black thread.

I'm looking at a dead man! he thought. *Oh Jesus, I'm looking at a dead man!* The sudden realisation hit him like an express train, and all at once he was noticing further details about the attackers. He was noticing how dishevelled they were, and how slowly and awkwardly they moved. He was noticing how sickly many of them looked, their complexions ranging from ghastly white to an awful greyish-green. He was noticing that one of the women attacking the young man had black, cancerous growths on her arms and legs. He was noticing that at the back of the crowd clustered around the ambulance was an eyeless child, shrivelled to the point of starvation. He was noticing that some of the attackers had skin so dried and puckered that their lips had drawn back from their mouths to reveal dark gums and yellow teeth. He was noticing bones poking through flesh; gaping wounds; canker and rot.

And he was noticing the smell. The high, sickening stench of a plague pit or charnel house.

'No,' he murmured, 'it's bloody impossible.'

He was so shocked that he didn't realise he had loosened his grip on his captive until the man suddenly twisted and lunged at him with a snarl, mouth gaping wide to bite.

'*Andy!*' screamed Dawn, but Andy was already jerking backwards. He heard the man's teeth clack on empty air.

Instantly the gatecrasher came at him again – and now the two men who had been eating the girl (the two *zombies*, Andy thought with a kind of horrified wonder) were rising to their feet, alerted by the commotion. They turned their heads. One of them let out a low, guttural moan, blood and drool spilling from slack lips.

Andy sidestepped as the zombie, its hands still handcuffed behind it, lunged again. He put up his hands to fend it off, and the zombie snapped at his fingers. Then Dawn was behind the creature, a clench-teethed look of revulsion and determination on her face. She jumped forward, shoving the zombie with all her might. Off-balance, it stumbled sideways and fell, crashing head-first into an overgrown rhododendron bush.

'Thanks,' Andy breathed, but already the two blood-drenched creatures who had killed the girl were stumbling towards them. One was wearing a checked shirt and jeans; the other had gore matted into its beard and was draped in a tattered white burial shroud.

Andy ducked as the zombie in the checked shirt made a swipe at him. He sensed rather than saw its clawed hand, fingernails caked with blood, passing over his head. Then Dawn was grabbing his arm, pulling him towards the gate.

'We've got to get away from here,' she said.

'But all those people in the house—'

'What are the two of us going to do against this lot? We'll have to call for back-up.'

Andy nodded, and they ran towards their car. In his peripheral vision he saw zombies registering them with whatever passed for cognisance in their dead brains. He was aware of the creatures abandoning their meals, converging on this new living prey with lurching, lumbering steps. He and Dawn dodged a girl in a green dress who had had part of her face torn away; a balding man in a mechanic's oily overall, his face bloated with rot.

As they neared the car, Andy fumbled for the key fob in his pocket, found it with sweaty fingers and pressed the button. He and Dawn wrenched the doors open and threw themselves inside. Andy rammed the key card into the slot and pressed the button which started the engine. All he could see around them were dead faces, slack and vacant, but also livid with a kind of relentless, idiot hunger. As he slammed the car into gear and they screeched away up the road, his only thought was that as soon as they'd requested back-up, he'd call Gwen. She and her Torchwood mates would know what was going on.

FIVE

Trystan Thomas spooned Horlicks into his mug, added a little milk and stirred vigorously. He glanced at the cooker, where more milk was heating up in a small pan for Sarah's hot chocolate. His wife hated Horlicks with a passion. She said it smelled like 'the Devil's vomit'. She always insisted Trys brush his teeth immediately after drinking it. In fact, she maintained that if it came to a choice between kissing a dog's bottom or her husband's Horlicksy mouth, she'd go for the dog every time.

They had been up watching a Tom Cruise movie, and now Sarah had hauled her bulk upstairs and was getting ready for bed. Trys still found it hard to get his head round the fact that in a matter of days they'd have a new addition to their household, a tiny human being who would be linked to them for the rest of their lives.

How many more nights would they spend in this house as a 'couple', Trys wondered. How much longer until they officially became a 'family'? And until *he* officially became a 'dad'?

Sometimes the thought frightened him. Sometimes he'd lie in bed, staring at the ceiling, with Sarah moving restlessly beside him, and he'd feel utterly overwhelmed. He'd feel too young to be a dad, not much more than a kid himself. How would he cope? What would he do? At those times he would get an overwhelming sense both of life rushing onwards, and of a door – the door leading back to his own youth and freedom – slamming firmly shut behind him.

But then in the morning, in the daylight, he would look at his beautiful pregnant wife, at the woman he loved, who had *their* baby growing inside her, and he would feel that surge of joy all over again, that sense of wonder and excitement.

The kettle and the milk boiled at the same time. Trys tipped the steaming milk into Sarah's favourite mug and added two big spoonfuls of instant hot chocolate. He was stirring it in when he heard his wife call his name. No, not call – *shout*. It was only one syllable, but Trys heard the urgency in it, the trace of panic.

He threw the spoon into the sink, and was out of the kitchen before it had even stopped clattering. Their house was small, two up, two down, with a narrow hallway. He bounded up the stairs two, three at a time, and burst into the bedroom, panting.

'What's up?'

Sarah was sitting on the edge of the bed with her nightie on and a look of alarm on her face. She was not conventionally attractive – her nose was a little too big, her eyes slightly too deep-set – but to Trys she was fascinating and unusual, and therefore twice as gorgeous as all those boringly pretty girls with their dyed hair and regular features.

'My waters have broken,' she said. 'It's starting, Trys.'

He noticed that the bed was wet, that there was a puddle on the carpet between her bare feet. 'Oh hell.'

'Phone Rianne,' instructed Sarah. 'Tell her we'll meet her at the hospital. My bag's in the hall. I just need you to help me get changed and get downstairs.'

'Course,' Trys said. He raised his hands, as if indicating she should stay put. 'Back in a minute.'

He ran downstairs, snatched up the telephone and punched in the mobile number of their midwife, Rianne Kilkenny, reading it from the post-it note that had been stuck to the wall for the past two weeks.

His mind was racing, thoughts tumbling over one another. Now that it had actually started, he couldn't quite believe it was happening. He thought of the abandoned mugs in the kitchen, one containing hot chocolate, the other a smooth paste of Horlicks powder and milk, and he thought to himself, *Next time I see those mugs, I'll be a dad.* It was amazing, incredible. He started to grin. He was still grinning when Rianne's gentle Irish voice said, 'Hello?'

***

Rianne switched her phone off and sighed – not that she *really* minded having to wait for the Thomases. It was simply that it had already been a very long day. One of her other 'ladies' (she preferred calling them that to 'patients' – it wasn't as if they were ill, after all) had just successfully given birth to a baby girl after a twenty-two-hour labour, and Rianne had been looking forward to going home and getting her head down for a while.

But that was part of her job. An occupational hazard. She could never predict *exactly* when her ladies' little darlings would choose to make their way into the world. Rianne might have two ladies whose dates were a month apart, but if one went into labour two weeks late and the other two weeks early, she might suddenly find she had twice the workload she was expecting – but also twice the joy and satisfaction as well.

She had been in Reception, heading towards the automatic glass doors that formed the hospital's main entrance, when the call had come in from Trystan Thomas. Now she might as well turn round and go straight back upstairs again – though she decided to get herself a bar of fruit and nut from the vending machine first. She deserved a treat.

Turning, she caught the eye of a girl slumped in one of the uncomfortable, metal-framed seats in Reception. The girl looked like a student – early twenties, pretty face, long dark hair. The girl smiled vaguely at her and nodded at the phone, which Rianne still held in her hand.

'Everything OK?' she asked.

'What? Oh, yes,' Rianne said. 'I'm just waiting for one of my ladies. She's gone into labour. I thought I might fuel up on chocolate before she arrived.'

'You a midwife, then?'

'I am, yes.' Rianne nodded down at the girl's leg. 'You look as though you've been in the wars.'

The girl was wearing jeans, one leg of which had been rolled up, and a bloodstained bandage wound inexpertly around her calf.

'I was a bit drunk. Put my foot through a plate-glass door. My mates reckoned I might need a few stitches.'

'I see. And where are your mates now?'

The girl gave a wry smile. 'Out clubbing, most probably.' Abruptly she thrust out a hand. 'I'm Nina Rogers.'

'Rianne Kilkenny,' Rianne said, taking the hand and shaking it. 'Well, good luck with the stitches. I'd better…' She gestured vaguely towards the vending machine.

'Yeah, you get on,' Nina said. 'Hope all the babies you deliver are healthy ones.'

Rianne smiled and was about to move away when she became aware of some sort of commotion by the main doors. She looked round, and was surprised to see a disparate group of people – some in dressing gowns and slippers over regulation hospital nightwear – hurrying in from outside. These were the smokers, a constant but ever-changing group of patients and visitors, who were forever to be found flocking around the main entrance like carrion crows. Now, however, they were heading back into the hospital en masse, apparently so eager to re-enter the warmth that they were almost tumbling over one another in their haste.

Rianne's first thought was that they must have been caught in a downpour, but when she glanced up at the sky through the glass doors she saw nothing but the same fine drizzle that had prevailed all evening. Then she noticed that many of the patients sitting on the rows of chairs closest to the entrance were slowly rising to their feet and turning their heads to look outside.

'What's going on?' Nina Rogers asked.

Rianne strained to see beyond the increasing number of people who were now bunched around the entrance doors, but their bobbing heads were obstructing her view.

'I've no idea,' she said.

Nina pushed herself awkwardly to her feet. 'Well, let's go and have a look, shall we?'

Rianne hesitated for just a second, then nodded and accompanied a hobbling Nina towards the main entrance. When they reached the crowd clustered around the doors, Nina tapped on the shoulder of a grey-haired woman with a long, heavily lined face. 'Excuse me, do you know what's happening?'

The woman turned. 'It's people,' she replied. 'They're coming from all over, surrounding the building. They reckon it's gangs.'

'Who do?' asked Rianne.

A thickset, bullet-headed man turned to address them. 'They'll be after the drugs,' he said.

'Has someone called the police?' another woman asked, anxiety straining her voice.

'Where's hospital security, that's what I'd like to know,' said a weaselly man with thinning hair and a brown cardigan.

There were further murmurs from the front of the crowd, a ripple of disquiet, like an electrical pulse.

'What's going on now?' Nina wanted to know, trying without success to peer over the heads of the knot of people in front of her.

An old lady with a powder puff of white hair and too much blusher, who was standing in front of the bullet-headed man, said over her shoulder, 'There's something wrong with them. They're not moving right.'

'Not moving right? Whatever do you mean?' Rianne asked. But the woman had turned away again now, and was absorbed in whatever was happening outside.

Rianne touched Nina's arm. 'I'm going upstairs,' she said. 'The windows at the top of the maternity ward overlook the car park. I'll have a better view from there.'

She expected Nina to nod and say goodbye, but instead the girl said firmly, 'I'll come with you.'

'Oh,' said Rianne, so taken aback by Nina's bluntness that instead of discouraging her, she found herself nodding. 'All right then. Come on.'

The two women crossed the foyer to the lifts. The maternity unit was on the fifth floor. They ascended silently and crossed to a set of double doors. As Rianne entered and held the doors open for the limping Nina,

Sister Felicity Andrews poked her head out of the nurses' station, a chocolate chunk cookie in her hand.

'Hello, Rianne,' she said pleasantly. 'Forgotten something?'

'Another of my ladies has gone into labour,' Rianne explained briskly. 'She's on her way in.' Before Sister Andrews could comment she added, 'Have you seen what's going on outside?'

'Outside? No, I...' Sister Andrews seemed to notice Nina for the first time. 'Who's this?'

Nina stepped forward, hand outstretched. 'Nina Rogers. It's OK, I'm just visiting.'

'Visiting? Well, it's not really—'

'Don't worry, Felicity, she's with me,' Rianne said.

Sister Andrews eyed Nina's bandaged leg doubtfully. 'Well, if you say so...'

The maternity unit more closely resembled a hotel suite than a medical facility. It comprised a wide central corridor with birthing rooms on one side and a series of ten-bed wards on the other. It had been designed with comfort and reassurance in mind, the walls and floors painted in soothing colours.

'Ward five is our intensive care unit,' Rianne explained, hurrying towards it. 'It's empty at the moment.'

They entered the room, which was lit by low-level lighting. There were only four beds in here, each enclosed within its own self-contained cubicle. On the wall opposite the door was a row of four waist-high windows. Rianne rushed across to them, her hands slapping the sill as she leaned forward to look outside, Nina trailing in her wake.

The car park in front of the hospital was on several levels and spread over a wide area. Each level was separated by clumps of bushes and young trees, and veined with pedestrian walkways. Usually at this hour there were not many people around; even vehicular traffic was infrequent. Yet tonight, despite the drizzly weather, there was movement everywhere – dozens of dark figures converging on the hospital. With a little chill of dread, Rianne realised that the white-haired old lady downstairs had been right: there *was* something odd, something *wrong*, about the way that the people were moving.

They were shuffling, lurching, dragging their feet. It was as though every single one of them was sleep-walking or drugged. Not only that, but many of them seemed to be holding their upper bodies stiffly – their shoulders hunched, their heads tilted at strange angles.

'What's the matter with them?' Nina asked wonderingly.

'I don't—' Rianne began, and then her eyes widened. 'Oh, sweet Jesus. Look there.'

She pointed at a thick clump of bushes directly below, which appeared to be nothing but a mass of black in the selectively illuminated darkness. Seconds earlier, she had seen a pair of arms emerge from the bushes and drag a head and shoulders into view. She had been wondering what was so wrong with the man that he had to crawl along the ground, when he had hauled the rest of himself into the light. She gaped now, unable to comprehend how little of him there was. His body simply stopped above what would have been his waist. He even appeared to be dragging a remnant of spine in his wake like a bony tail.

Rianne felt Nina's hand tighten on her arm. The girl's eyes were as wide as she imagined her own to be.

'That *is* impossible, isn't it?' she said. 'He can't survive like that, can he?'

'Evidently he can,' Rianne said, and felt the sudden appalling urge to giggle.

More of the shuffling figures were now emerging from the shadows, into the light that was bleeding from the hospital. As they did so, both women were horrified to see that the crawling man was not alone in his affliction. Too many of the figures were dressed in rags; too many were stick-thin; too many were hideously misshapen or lacking limbs.

'What *is* this?' Nina murmured. 'Amputees' outing?'

'They look like they've been in a battle,' said Rianne. 'The walking wounded.'

The words were barely out of her mouth when twin headlamps swept into the car park entrance behind the shuffling army – a late patient or visitor, Rianne thought. Or perhaps a member of staff about to start the graveyard shift.

The car swept down the curving approach road, as though its driver was in a hurry and unaware of the crowd in his path.

'He's going to hit someone,' Nina said, her hand once again tightening on Rianne's arm.

And then with a screech of brakes the car stopped.

None of the figures had flinched or leaped aside as the vehicle bore down on them. Even now, they didn't move to the side of the road to allow the car through, as any normal person would have done.

The car seemed to pause for a moment, dark and sleek, like a big cat sizing up its prey – and then the driver's door flew open and a man scrambled out. Neither Rianne nor Nina could tell from their vantage point what the man was saying, but it was clear from his body language that he was not happy. He marched towards the three or four figures in the path of his car, waving his arms, head jerking as he shouted. The two women saw a couple of the shuffling figures stumble to a halt, saw them turn clumsily to face the furious man.

Then they saw the man stop dead, his arms dropping to his sides and, even from five floors up, Rianne could have sworn she could see the man's eyes widen in horror and shock.

Next moment the man was running back to his car, and the figures were lurching after him. Rianne felt a leap of fear in her chest for the man's safety, but she told herself that he would surely be fast enough to outrun his shuffling pursuers; that he would surely have time to make it back to his car, shut and lock the door, and reverse to safety before they had covered even half the distance.

Legs rigid, hands gripping the windowsill, she was urging the man to get away when she saw two black figures, as if formed from the darkness, step out of the bushes on either side of him. The figures were between the man and his car. He stopped, momentarily uncertain what to do, where to go. Then he dodged to his left, as if to plunge into the bushes himself, to make his escape that way – and another figure, tall and gangly and skeletal, stepped from the shadowy clump of foliage right into his path, and clawed with twig-spiny fingers at the man's face.

The man hurled himself backwards, pinwheeling his arms, trying desperately to maintain his balance. Rianne rose up on her toes, urging him to stay on his feet; Nina's grip on her arm tightened again, tightened enough to bruise. Both women let out a joint cry of despair as the man lost his struggle, tumbling on to his backside, his head hitting the ground hard. Within seconds the lurching, malformed creatures were on him, rending and tearing and clawing. Nina expelled a shrieking sob and turned away, reaching out instinctively for comfort. She and Rianne clung to each other, shocked and uncomprehending.

It was a long time before either of them could speak.

'A *zombie*,' Rhys said incredulously. 'A bloody *zombie*, for Christ's sake!'

'We don't *know* that's what it was,' Gwen said. 'Let's not jump to conclusions.'

They were in the car, heading through the streets of Grangetown towards Corporation Road. After calling Jack, they had stopped only to get properly dressed and for Gwen to grab some extra ammunition. Now they were on their way to the Hub to liaise with Jack and Ianto.

'*Jack's* jumping to conclusions,' Rhys pointed out. 'Zombie attack, *he* said. Zombie attack on Cardiff. Sounds like a computer game.'

Gwen smiled. 'Jack likes to be dramatic.'

'*Jesus!*' Rhys exclaimed as a police car suddenly rocketed past them, siren screaming and lights going like crazy. Their own Saab rocked slightly in the slipstream. 'Wonder where he's going in such a hurry.'

Before Gwen could reply, her phone rang. She answered it on the second ring. 'Jack?'

She listened for a moment, frowned in puzzlement, and then shot a glance at Rhys. 'Andy, what are you—'

Rhys grinned wickedly. 'Not still mooning after you, is he?' he said, loudly enough to be overheard.

Still frowning, Gwen put a hand on Rhys's arm and gave a little shake of the head. Rhys could tell from her expression that whatever Andy was telling her was serious.

'You're joking me,' she said. And, 'Oh my God.' And, 'OK, Andy, thanks… No, you get her to hospital… I'm on my way to meet them now, as a matter of fact… Yeah, see you.'

She pocketed the phone and puffed out her cheeks, as though exhaling a long-held breath.

'What?' Rhys asked.

'It's everywhere,' she said, and there was a hushed tone to her voice which chilled Rhys to the core. She told him what Andy had told her – about zombies attacking a group of partygoers in Gabalfa, about how his partner had been bitten and was bleeding badly. 'This is mad,' she said. 'It's just… mad.'

'Madder than aliens?' Rhys said.

'Yes!' she snapped, as though affronted by the sheer outrageousness of what was happening. 'Aliens I can understand, but *zombies*? It doesn't make sense.'

Rhys was about to reply when his unspoken words were superseded by an ear-splitting howl of brakes and a shockingly loud crash from somewhere ahead. He reacted as though a pedestrian had stepped out in front of the car, hunching his shoulders and stamping on the brakes, arms rigid as he clenched the steering wheel.

'What the hell was *that*?' he said.

'Car crash?' suggested Gwen.

'Sounded like a bloody building falling down.'

'Let's check it out, shall we?'

He gave a short nod, put the car into gear and eased it forward.

'I think it came from up there,' Gwen said, pointing at the right turn into Bradford Street.

Rhys nodded again and turned into the road that Gwen had indicated.

'Oh my God,' she breathed.

Less than ten metres ahead of them, the police car

that had gone screaming past a few minutes earlier was embedded in the now-demolished garden wall of a suburban house. Judging by the thick black skid-marks on the road, visible in the light of the Saab's headlamps, the car had swerved out of control, mounted the pavement and smashed at some speed into the waist-high stone barrier. However it was wasn't the crumpled car, nor even the sight of its two unconscious, bloodstained occupants, that was responsible for Gwen's shocked exhalation.

The street was swarming with zombies. Dozens of them shuffled and lurched in apparently random directions. Though even as Gwen and Rhys gaped in horror and disbelief, the undead began to turn as one, to converge with slow and remorseless purpose on the wrecked car and its stricken occupants.

SIX

'That's interesting,' Ianto said.

He and Jack had just entered the Hub through the revolving cog-wheel door, which was now rolling back into place behind them. They were here to check data, take readings, try to find some rhyme and reason for what was happening – and thus, they hoped, formulate a strategy to combat it.

Jack was in the lead, striding along the iron walkway towards the central work area, where a bank of interlinked computers and readout screens assimilated and displayed information.

Now he glanced over his shoulder to see that Ianto had come to a halt, his attention elsewhere.

'What is?' Jack asked.

Ianto indicated a work bench tucked into an alcove

close to the steps leading down to the Autopsy Room. On the bench was a shattered chunk of what looked to have once been a football-sized orb of some silvery, iridescent material. The orb fragment, which rippled gently with light, was nestled within a complex cradle of monitoring equipment, not unlike a miniature version of the work station area. Ianto's attention was snagged by a scrolling bank of data on a monitor screen.

'These enzyme readings are going through the roof,' he said.

'Meaning?'

'Meaning that the pod's rate of regeneration is increasing exponentially.'

Jack arched an eyebrow. He appreciated Ianto's efforts to step into the considerable breach left by the deaths of Owen and Tosh, but he couldn't deny that the extra workload his friend and colleague had recently taken on affected his focus on occasion. Even the normally exceptional standard of Ianto's coffee had slipped a little these past months. Not that Jack would have said anything. Ianto would have been devastated.

'Your point being?'

Ianto shrugged. 'It's just interesting, that's all. Didn't I already say that?'

'You did,' Jack acknowledged, 'and much as I admire your ability to multitask, I really think we need to focus on the matter in hand.' He smiled to show his words were not intended as a reprimand, and swept away, resuming his long-legged stride towards the Rift-monitoring equipment, which was invariably their first port of call in an emergency, and the technological heart of the Hub.

By the time Ianto had joined him, Jack was hopping from screen to screen, poring over the ever-shifting banks of figures and diagrams.

'Look at this,' he said, jabbing at a schematic of a dome-like structure looming over a gridded relief map of the city.

Ianto leaned forward, automatically smoothing down his tie with his hand. 'What is it? Some kind of energy barrier?'

'A *time* energy barrier,' Jack corrected. 'Highly sophisticated. This is not good.'

'So we're sealed in?'

'Like rats in a cage. Nothing can enter or leave the city. It's gonna play havoc with the gene pool.'

Ianto didn't laugh, but raised his eyebrows to acknowledge the quip. 'What about the visitors?'

Jack moved to another computer, tapped out a few directions on the keyboard, and a more detailed street map of the city flashed up on a large, free-standing flatscreen a few metres away. This map, etched in ice-blue light, was speckled with random clusters of ant-like blips. Even as Ianto watched, more blips appeared, seemingly from nowhere.

'Zombies,' Jack said. Ianto winced. 'As you can see, they're just… popping into existence all over.'

'They're coming through the Rift, you mean?'

'You'd think *so*, wouldn't you?' Jack shook his head.

'But here's the weird thing. There are no signs of recent Rift activity.'

Ianto stared at him. 'But that's impossible.'

'All the same…' Jack shrugged, waving a hand at the screen, as if to say: *Here's the evidence. Deal with it.*

Ianto crossed back to the computer readouts, stared at them, matching one to the other, trying to make sense of what they were telling him. Finally he said, 'But according to these readings, each of the visitors does possess a *residual* trace of Rift energy. It's almost as if…'

He tailed off, seeking an explanation. Jack nodded, picking up his train of thought. 'As if the zombies haven't actually come *through* the Rift, and yet are still linked to it in some way.'

Ianto looked bewildered. 'But that doesn't make sense. Does it?'

'Maybe not,' Jack said, and grinned suddenly. 'But when all's said and done, what the hell *does* make sense in this crazy universe of ours?'

Ianto looked thoughtful, and then sighed. 'Are you thinking what I'm thinking?'

'Reckon I am,' Jack said, adopting a good-ole-boy accent. 'Let's you and me head on out into them there badlands and go bag us a cotton-pickin' zombie.'

'Remember what Rianne told you,' Trys said. 'Breathe through the pain.'

Sarah Thomas scowled at her husband. She was slumped in the passenger seat of their Passat, hands gently stroking her swollen belly. The contractions were more frequent now, and more acute.

'I *am* breathing through the pain,' she said through gritted teeth. 'You just concentrate on driving.'

She was being snappy, but Trys could hardly blame her. He said nothing, fixing his eyes back on the road. He was driving steadily now, after a panicky start. Soon after they had set off, Sarah had put a hand on his arm and said, 'Calm down, Trys. It's more important to get us there in one piece than it is to break the land-speed record.'

'Sorry,' he had replied. 'I'm not handling this very well, am I?'

'You're doing fine,' she'd told him, as if *he* was the one about to give birth. 'There's no one else I'd rather be with tonight.'

One thing Trys was thankful for was that at this hour the suburban roads leading to the hospital were blessedly quiet. Aside from a couple of drunks they had seen lurching along the pavement, there was no one about.

'We'll be there soon,' he told her. 'How you doing, love?'

'Doing fine,' she said, and then her weary smile turned into a look of alarm. 'Trys, watch out!'

Trys had only glanced away from the road for a split second. Now he turned back, and was astonished to see that he was bearing down on a quartet of figures crouched in the path of his headlights. Fortunately the figures were still far enough away that he had plenty of time to react. He eased his foot gently down on the brake and gave a warning bip of his horn. He expected the figures to look up, perhaps acknowledge him with a wave and move aside, but they remained where they were, as if oblivious to the car's presence. As the Passat got closer to them, slowing all the while, Trys realised that the figures were crouching *over* something, that a dark shape was lying in the road at their feet.

'Looks as though someone's hurt,' he said, slowing to a stop.

Even now, in the glare of the headlights, the figures did not respond. Sarah shifted in the passenger seat, one hand spread protectively over her belly.

'More likely drunk,' she said. 'Or maybe this lot have mugged the guy in the road and they're going through his pockets.'

'Always so cynical,' Trys said with a wry smile.

'No, just realistic,' replied Sarah bluntly. 'Not everyone's as nice as you, you know, Trys.'

'I'm aware of that,' he said, more sharply than he intended. 'I'm not an idiot.'

'I never said you were.' Then her voice and face softened. 'Come on, let's just get out of here. Back up and take the next road. It won't make any difference.'

'We can't leave someone lying injured in the street,' he said. 'He might need urgent medical attention.'

'*I* need urgent medical attention,' Sarah said. 'I'm having our baby, remember.'

'I'll just find out what's going on,' Trys said, reaching for the door handle. 'I won't be a minute.'

'No, Trys, don't.' Sarah grabbed her husband's arm.

He looked at her quizzically. 'Why not?'

'I've just got a bad feeling about this. It could be a trap.'

'I'll stay close to the car,' he assured her. 'Don't worry, I'll be fine.' He laid his hand over hers and stroked it gently. 'The sooner I find out, the sooner we can go.'

Reluctantly she let go of him. 'All right, but be careful. And we're not giving anyone a lift to the hospital.'

He raised a hand in agreement and got out of the car. The soft drizzle was like the touch of ghostly fingertips on his skin.

'Excuse me,' he said, taking a few steps forward. Even now the crouching figures failed to respond to him. He stepped closer, until he was standing parallel with the front of the Passat. Drizzle filled the white beams of the headlights like silver static. Clearing his throat and raising his voice, Trys tried again. 'Excuse me.'

This time one of the figures seemed to register his presence. It stiffened a little, hunching its shoulders. Trys took another couple of steps forward, until he was standing partially in the beam of one of the headlights, fracturing and narrowing it.

'Is everything OK?' he asked. 'Do you need help?'

On unsteady legs, the figure which had hunched its shoulders began to rise from its crouched position. Slowly it turned towards him. The instant the light fell on its face, Trys felt a jolt of shock and fear lance down through his body.

The figure had no eyes. Just black holes where its eyes had once been. Its withered skin, the colour of old leaves, clung tightly to the skull beneath. Worst of all, it had a piece of raw, ragged meat, oozing blood, dangling from its mouth.

Trys staggered backwards. All at once his limbs felt alien, unresponsive, his thoughts soft and soupy, as though he was about to faint. He blinked, trying to focus, and as the other figures began to rise he saw clearly for the first time what they had been crouching over.

It was a human body, so horribly mangled that its sex was impossible to determine. It had been gutted, the stomach ripped open, the entrails pulled out and strewn across the tarmac. Clearly the creatures, the ghouls – Trys felt his mind skidding away from the undeniable fact that the figures now closing slowly in on him were *zombies* – had been feasting on it. Their hands were gloved in blood, their hideous dead faces masked in offal. One of the zombies was a teenage girl in a gore-spattered Girls Aloud T-shirt, who even now was chewing on one of the victim's feet.

The backs of Trys's thighs bumped against the car. Surprised, his legs folded forward at the knees, causing him to sit on the bonnet. Even in his dreamy disbelief he was aware of how cold and wet the metal was through the seat of his jeans. He heard banging behind him and turned his head. Despite the obstruction of her belly, Sarah was leaning forwards, her face contorted with panic, her fist bashing the inside of the windscreen.

She was mouthing at him, and all at once it was as though his senses had unblocked, and suddenly he could hear her words.

'*Get in!*' she was screaming. '*Get in! Get in!*'

It was enough to snap Trys out of his trance. He turned and slithered across and around the bonnet, the zombies just behind him. His foot skidded from under him on the slippery pavement, but he managed to regain his balance. He reached for the door handle and grabbed it.

But before he could pull it open, he heard a sighing groan behind him, and a hand came down on his shoulder. Despite the emaciated state of his pursuer, the thing's grip was fierce, immovable. Trys yelped as knife-sharp fingers dug through the fabric of his jacket and into his flesh. Then he felt something worse – a hot, searing pain just above his elbow. He glanced behind him and screamed. The teenage girl had cast aside the gnawed foot and was sinking her teeth into the meat of his arm.

Trys fought frantically, trying to struggle free, but the other zombies were on him now, one biting into his shoulder, another latching onto his back. He thought of Sarah, of his unborn baby, of how he had to somehow escape from this because he had to drive his wife to hospital, had to spend the rest of his life being a dad to his son or daughter. He looked through the car window and saw Sarah's screaming, hysterical face, and he wanted to tell her that he was sorry, that she was right, that he should never have got out of the car, that he should have listened to her. He could feel hot, hot pain spreading across the back of his body; could feel the shocking wetness of his own blood running down his back and soaking through his clothes. Fighting the threat of unconsciousness, he took a renewed grip on the handle and managed to yank the driver's door a little way open.

Like wailing banshees escaping from a box, Sarah's terrible, high-pitched screams came tearing out of the car. Instantly Trys realised his mistake, realised that all he had achieved was to deflect the zombies' attention away from him and onto his wife. Whether it was her screams or the baby inside her which attracted them, Trys had no idea, but suddenly he felt himself released, pushed aside, like a bag of rubbish.

He tried to stay on his feet, determined to defend his wife and unborn child to his last breath, but his body wouldn't respond. As consciousness slipped away, he felt his legs folding under him, felt himself sliding down the side of the car, his hands squeaking as he tried vainly to get a grip on the wet metal. Then he was lying in the gutter, the drizzle speckling his upturned face. The last thing he heard as he lay there, as the searing pain of his injuries seemed to exude a darkness which threatened to overwhelm him, was Sarah's voice, raggedly screaming his name over and over again.

SEVEN

'We've got to help them, Rhys,' Gwen said, producing her gun for the second time that night.

'How?' Rhys wanted to know. 'There's dozens of the buggers.'

Gwen's eyes were blazing. 'We have to try.'

Rhys gave a short nod, knowing she was right, and put his foot down.

The car shot forward, towards the crumpled police car and the knot of zombies converging on it. Gwen could see that the driver of the vehicle was still unconscious, his head resting on the steering wheel, blood running down his face. However, his partner was starting to come to, lifting his head groggily, looking around. All at once Gwen saw him snap alert as he took in the true nature of the creatures surrounding him. She saw him trying frantically to extricate himself from the smashed-up vehicle. She saw the first of the zombies – a purple-faced woman in a floral-patterned dress who was dragging one leg behind her – arrive at the car and reach in through the shattered passenger window. She heard the man scream—

—and it was then that another zombie leaped from between two parked cars on their left and crashed onto their bonnet.

Rhys swore, the car slewing from left to right. The zombie spread-eagled on their bonnet snarled at them, pressing its face to the window. It was a young man with blond streaks in his spiky hair and skin like black-veined marble. His eyes were completely white, and black, tar-like drool was spilling from his open mouth.

Rhys couldn't see where he was going. The zombie slapped the windscreen with a hand from which two of the fingers had rotted away, leaving a smeary mark.

Gwen unclipped her seatbelt, wound down her window and leaned out, levelling her gun, intending to blast the zombie off the car. Then she saw that they were veering towards a tree on the pavement and ducked back inside.

'*Rhys!*' she screamed.

Too late he slammed on the brakes. The zombie on their bonnet slithered off in a tangle of arms and legs. There was a sickening crunch and a sideways lurch as they ran over it. Gwen and Rhys both yelled, as if on a fairground ride, as the car skidded, out of control. Gwen managed to clip her seatbelt back into place a split second before they slewed sideways into a line of parked cars. There was a crunching, jolting impact, and then silence.

Gwen's head was ringing. She opened her mouth, rotating her jaw. Already her brain was working, assessing the damage to her body. She'd whacked her hip and her shoulder badly enough to bruise, but she'd be all right. Trying to blink her vision back into some sort of equilibrium, she glanced across at Rhys. He was sitting upright, eyes closed.

'Rhys? Are you OK?'

He opened his eyes. 'Have we stopped?'

'Are you OK?' she repeated urgently.

'Yeah, I'm fine. You?'

She nodded, then wished she hadn't as a sharp but momentary pain lanced through her neck. 'Start the car again,' she said. 'We're sitting targets here.'

Rhys tried the ignition. The car wheezed and coughed, then died. He waited a few seconds, and then tried again, with the same result. The third time nothing happened at all.

'It's knackered,' he said. 'Bloody company car an' all.'

'Oh, that's brilliant, that is,' Gwen exclaimed. She glanced out through the cracked windscreen. The majority of zombies were still milling around the police car, from which the terrified screams of its occupant had now ominously ceased. One or two, though, were shuffling towards them.

'We have to get out,' she said.

Rhys tried his door, but it was buckled and jammed up hard against the vehicle they had collided with. 'I'll have to get out your side,' he said.

Gwen threw her door open and scrambled out, clutching her gun and gritting her teeth against the pain in her hip. She looked around, and was horrified to see that the front doors of houses were now opening up and down the street, and that local residents were venturing out to see what the commotion was. Even as she watched, Gwen saw two zombies go blundering up a garden path towards an old lady who was silhouetted in her doorway. Wearing a pink nightgown, the lady held a cat in her arms, and seemed to be rooted to the spot in terror.

'*Back inside, all of you!*' Gwen yelled. '*And lock your doors! This is an emergency situation!*'

As if to emphasise the fact, the zombies reached the old lady and grabbed her. The cat fell yowling from her arms and streaked away as one of the zombies, a fat man in a blood and grime-stained traffic warden's uniform, tore her throat out. People began to scream. Some fled inside and slammed their doors. Just as many, however, ran *away* from their houses, as if intending to rush to the old lady's aid.

Gwen fired her gun into the air. The sound was shockingly loud in the suburban street.

'*Go back inside!*' she shouted again. '*Secure your doors and windows, and stay there until you're told it's safe to come out!*'

Behind her, Rhys had scrambled across the front seats of the car and was now sliding forward out of the passenger door, hands reaching down to the ground to support his weight.

'Er... Gwen,' he said.

She turned and saw a zombie appear around the back of the car, a tall, thin woman with an untidy beehive of black hair, wearing what appeared to be a silk ball gown. Part of the woman's bottom lip had been torn away, which made her look as though she was baring her teeth like a dog. Another three steps and she would have been close enough to Rhys to grab him.

Without hesitation, Gwen raised her gun and fired. The woman was thrown backwards as a hole, leaking thick, blackish blood, appeared in the centre of her chest. As Gwen pulled Rhys out of the car and helped him to his feet, the woman pushed herself awkwardly upright once more. Gwen shot her a second time. This time the bullet hit her in the shoulder and spun her around. Once again, however, like a boxer that keeps getting hit but won't stay down, she clambered to her feet.

'You have to shoot them in the head,' Rhys said.

Gwen blinked at him. 'What?'

'That's what they always do in the movies. To kill them you have to shoot them in the head, destroy their brains.'

'This *isn't* the movies, Rhys,' Gwen snapped.

'Just *try it*,' he ordered.

She made an exasperated sound, but as the woman lurched towards them again, she raised her gun, aiming higher this time, and pulled the trigger.

The top half of the woman's head blew away, taking a good chunk of her beehive hairdo with it. With a look almost of surprise, she crumpled to the ground, a dead weight. Her body twitched for a moment and then was still.

'See,' Rhys said smugly.

'Don't gloat, Rhys,' Gwen replied. 'It's not attractive.'

She ran towards the police car, gun held out before her. Zombies converged from all sides, but Gwen twisted and turned, shooting them in the head. Rhys ran along behind her, crouching low, wishing he had a gun too. He had never fired one in his life, and wasn't even sure whether he would be able to bring himself to point one at a person – even a dead person – and pull the trigger, but he wished he had one all the same.

A crowd of maybe three dozen zombies were still milling around the wrecked vehicle, but as Gwen and Rhys approached they started to peel away, to turn round, alerted by whatever weird senses they possessed to the proximity of live meat. Calmly and methodically, Gwen began to take them out one by one. Her reactions were fast, her movements fluid, but even so the sheer number of the creatures, slow though they were, was forcing her and Rhys to retreat.

'We've got to find a way through,' Gwen muttered between shots.

Rhys's ears were ringing from the gunfire, but he heard her words and knew how desperate she was to help the policemen. Enough of the zombies had peeled away from the vehicle now, however, for him to be able to see inside it. It was abundantly clear to him that both officers were way beyond help. There was very little left of either of them.

'It's too late,' he said softly. Gwen appeared not to hear him. She was still firing, her teeth clenched, dark eyes full of fury. Rhys put his hand on her shoulder and raised his voice. 'It's too late, love. They're both dead.'

She glanced at him, anguish on her face.

'And if we don't get away from here, we'll be joining them,' he added.

Gwen nodded, though not before shooting a blonde-haired zombie in a nurse's uniform, who was holding something red and oozing that was leaving a trail on the road behind her. 'I know,' she muttered.

Rhys grabbed her free hand. 'Then let's go.'

They ran back along the street, Gwen still shooting, Rhys dodging clumsily flailing arms and clutching hands. When they came parallel with the car, he stopped abruptly, almost yanking Gwen's arm off.

'Hang on a sec,' he said.

'What are you doing, Rhys?' Gwen demanded in exasperation. '*Come on.*'

'I need a weapon too,' he said. 'Give me ten seconds.' He ran round to the back of the car and popped the boot open. Rummaging inside, he drew out what at first Gwen thought was a sword, but then realised was a golf club.

'See?' he said, hefting the club in his hand. 'Not a complete waste of money, after all.'

Gwen rolled her eyes. Rhys had bought the clubs on eBay, with the intention of taking up golf. After a couple of rounds at their local course, however, he had decided he liked neither the game nor the people who played it, and the clubs had been gathering dust in the boot of the car ever since.

He grinned at her, reached up and pushed down the boot – which revealed a bespectacled, middle-aged man with a rotting, greenish face. The man had shuffled up the pavement on Rhys's blindside and was now less than a metre away from him.

'*Rhys!*' Gwen screamed, but he didn't need the warning. Moving with remarkable agility for a man forty pounds above his optimum weight, he spun round and buried the business end of the club in the zombie's forehead.

The zombie's eyes rolled up and it collapsed, the head of the club coming free with a gristly tearing sound as it fell. Rhys stared at the creature in a kind of wonder, and then looked at the head of the club, which was covered with a mess of blood and grey-green gloop.

'Can we go now?' Gwen asked impatiently.

'Right behind you, sweetheart,' said Rhys.

Sophie and Kirsty were sitting in the back of a cab on Bute Street, en route to Oceana on Greyfriars Road. Both girls were feeling mellow, tapping their feet and moving their bodies to the seventies funk which filled the car. The traffic lights were on red and the engine was idling. The cab driver was called Winston, and he'd already told them all about his fortieth birthday a month ago, which he had celebrated by visiting his extended family in Jamaica. Now Winston was taking the opportunity to have a quick roll-up, blowing blue-grey smoke out of his open window. Drizzle sheened the streets and blurred the light from the overhead lamps. The pubs had shut and there were very few people around.

'You girls ain't too cold with the window open?' Winston said between puffs on his straw-thin cigarette.

'No, we're fine,' said Sophie, though in truth she *was* a bit cold; she had goose bumps on her bare arms.

'I'm never cold,' Kirsty said, and touched her forearm with the tip of an index finger, making a *tsss* sound. 'I'm always *hot.*'

Winston chuckled. 'I can believe it. So how come you girls are out partyin' so late at night? Ain't you got work in the mornin'?'

Kirsty leaned forward, resting her arm on the back of his seat. 'No, we're—' she began.

And at that moment a chalk-white hand with black fingernails reached in through the driver's side window and ripped Winston's face off.

It happened in an instant. The hand seemed simply to dig its fingers into the soft flesh beneath Winston's jaw and peel off his skin like a balaclava. Winston fell backwards without a sound, sprawling across the front seats, his roll-up still held daintily between the forefinger and second finger of his right hand. Blood fountained from his severed jugular vein, an arterial spray which drenched Kirsty in an instant. She screamed and threw up her hands. All Sophie could do was gape in utter disbelief.

Then the door next to Kirsty was wrenched open, and half a dozen hands shot into the car, grabbed hold of the screaming girl and dragged her out. Sophie couldn't believe what was happening, couldn't believe that less than ten seconds ago she, Kirsty and Winston had been chatting and listening to music. She sat there, frozen in terror, as she heard Kirsty's screams rise in pitch and agony, until they became almost too unbearable to listen to. 'No!' Kirsty was screaming. 'No, please…' There was a final gurgling scream and then silence.

Shaking from head to foot, her sparkly top speckled with Winston's blood, Sophie reached for the door handle. At first she wasn't sure she even had the strength to turn it. Then the door clicked open and she all but fell into the road. She got up, sobbing, her legs shaky and weak, her stomach juddering, as if she was frozen to the core. She looked over the roof of the car and saw a group of… things, tearing at something that was covered in blood. Something that no longer looked human. Something that Sophie refused to believe had been her best friend less than a minute before.

Head spinning, her breathing coming in sobbing, shuddering gulps, she tottered away on her high heels. After a few steps she paused to kick them off, and then, with the chill wetness of the ground soaking into her stockinged feet, she ran.

***

98

'Left here, Jack,' Ianto said.

Jack swung the SUV into the sharp turn without even slowing. The tyres made a screeching hiss on the wet tarmac.

'Whoa there, Mr Testosterone,' Ianto said drily. 'There's no need to impress *me* with your crazy stunt driving.'

'Never walk when you can run, Ianto,' Jack said heartily.

'Never die when you can live,' Ianto muttered, and then added, 'Oh, I was forgetting – *you* don't.'

They were 'zombie-hunting', as Jack kept insisting on calling it, the monitoring equipment inside the SUV acting as a kind of 'zombie' satnav. Ianto was using the readings to give Jack directions; only problem was, the 'zombies' – whether by accident or through some kind of flocking instinct – tended to congregate in large groups, and that was something they were trying to avoid. They were in Trowbridge, on the trail of a quartet of the creatures, which appeared to have been stationary for the last five minutes or so. Trowbridge was an area of tight suburban streets and public housing, though it was presently undergoing something of a facelift. The 'zombies' – or at least their Rift traces – had been detected on a road with pre-war housing on one side and a building site (which would soon become desirable new dwellings) on the other.

'First right,' Ianto said, and raised his eyebrows when the wheels on the passenger side of the SUV briefly left the road as Jack took the turn. A dozen metres ahead, parked in the middle of the road, was a blue Passat with its lights on. Jack drove towards it at speed, as if he expected it to simply get out of his way.

'Brake,' Ianto said mildly.

Jack hit the brakes, and the SUV came to a halt mere centimetres from the Passat's rear bumper. Ianto was about to deliver a caustic comment when he saw what Jack had already seen. A man was lying in the gutter beside the car, whilst four figures – little more than dark, bobbing shapes – clawed and scrabbled and thumped at the vehicle, trying to gain access. Ianto supposed there was someone inside that the attackers were trying to get to, but from here he couldn't tell. Jack was already throwing his door open, drawing his Webley, Ianto only a couple of seconds behind him.

'Is this a private party or can anyone join in?' Jack shouted. He was grinning, but his gun arm was raised and ramrod-straight.

'Oh, my,' Ianto breathed as the group of figures clustered around the car turned to face them. It was the first time he had seen a 'zombie', but he had to admit their appearance was all-too familiar. Each of them looked as though they had stepped straight off the set of a low-budget horror movie. Ragged, stained clothes; discoloured skin; blank expressions – it was all there. The creatures ticked all the boxes, even in terms of their various stages of decomposition. One was almost skeletal, one ghostly-white, another greenish and bloated. Plus there was a girl, maybe twelve or thirteen years old, who looked as though she could have died yesterday. The girl, her chin and T-shirt caked in blood, her dead eyes sheened with an almost silvery glaze, hissed and crouched. The others moaned and shuffled.

'We'll take *her*,' Jack said to Ianto.

'Because she's the… prettiest?' Ianto ventured.

Jack shot him a look. 'Come on, Ianto, even *I'm* not *that* shallow. I was thinking more that she wouldn't smell as bad as her buddies.'

Ianto cocked an eyebrow, as if he didn't believe a word of it. 'What about the others?'

'We've got live people in peril here,' Jack said, nodding at the car, inside which they could now see a woman's terrified face peering at them. 'We take them out.'

'Just kill them, you mean?'

'Why not? They're dead already.'

Seemingly oblivious to the weapons that Jack and Ianto were pointing at them, the creatures had now halved the distance between the car and the two men. Without further preamble, Jack raised his Webley and shot the skeletal zombie through the head. Most of its skull blew away like old tree bark and it dropped unceremoniously to the ground.

Gritting his teeth, Ianto shot a balding man with a ginger moustache and splotches of black mould on his greenish skin. The bullet hit the man in the chest, but he simply went down on one knee with a wheeze of escaping air, then stood up again.

'You need to finish them with a head shot,' Jack said,

circling round to get a better aim at the third zombie, a chubby guy in what must once have been a nice suit.

'How do you know that?' Ianto asked.

'Believe me, when you've been around as long as I have, you get through a hell of a lot of movies.'

Ianto shook his head, but raised his gun and shot the balding man between the eyes. There was a spurt of thin blood and the man fell over backwards, his skull hitting the pavement with a sound like a dropped coconut.

'This doesn't feel right,' Ianto said. 'These were people once.'

'And now they're just animated cadavers,' said Jack, dropping the guy in the suit with a single shot. 'Think of them as glove puppets.'

'Thanks,' said Ianto. 'That makes me feel a lot better.'

'Hey,' Jack said, circling around to the other side of the car, head snapping from left to right. 'Where'd the girl go?'

Ianto saw a suggestion of movement in the building site across the road, a shadow flitting between the dumper trucks and excavators.

'There,' he said, pointing.

'I see her,' said Jack. He was already running, coat flying behind him. 'I'll get the girl, you look after the people here. Back in five.'

He was gone before Ianto could argue.

'Hang on,' panted Rhys.

He had fallen half a dozen metres behind Gwen, who

stopped to let him catch up. His face was red and his forehead was beaded with either sweat or drizzle. His hair stood up in wet spikes.

'You all right, love?' Gwen asked.

He thumped to a halt beside her, putting out a hand to lean against the wall. Gasping, he said, 'You know me, sweetheart. I'm built for endurance, not speed.'

She smiled and rubbed his shoulder supportively. 'We'll have a breather. I reckon we're safe for now.'

They had run, and then jogged, from Bradford Street to Corporation Road, and across Clarence Bridge. Gwen had been hoping they'd be able to make it all the way along James Street to Roald Dahl Plass, where the Hub was located, but on the opposite side of the bridge they had stumbled across a group of about ten zombies shuffling towards them. Knackered though he was, Rhys had been willing to batter his way through with his trusty golf club, but Gwen had decided there was nothing to be gained in taking unnecessary risks. So they had taken a detour along Clarence Embankment and through the tight cluster of residential streets which branched off from it. They were now in a quiet alley linking Harrowby Lane to Harrowby Street, high walls on either side of them.

Rhys leaned against one of the walls with a groan and mopped his brow. 'When I said I wanted some action this evening, this isn't quite what I meant.'

Gwen snorted a brief laugh. 'I wonder what's causing this,' she mused.

'In the movies it's always chemicals or radiation or something,' said Rhys.

She pulled a face. 'That's just daft.'

'This whole situation is daft, if you ask me. I mean, where are all these zombies coming from? Up out of the ground? Hospitals? Morgues?'

Gwen looked thoughtful, then pulled out her phone. 'I'll call Jack, see if he's found out anything.'

She fast-dialled him. He answered on the first ring. 'Hey, Jack, what's going on?'

'I'm zombie-hunting,' he said. His voice was hushed, but he sounded perversely as if he was enjoying himself.

'Where are you?'

'Somewhere in Trowbridge.'

'So you're not at the Hub?'

'What would be the point of zombie-hunting in the Hub?'

Gwen shook her head at the playful but unmistakable disdain in his voice. 'Yeah, sorry. Ignore me. My thoughts are all over the place.'

'Where are *you*?' Jack asked.

Quickly, Gwen filled him in on what had been happening to her and Rhys, and their present location.

'But listen, Jack,' she said, 'these things are everywhere. This is bigger than we can handle.' She hesitated a moment, then said, 'I'm thinking we need outside help on this. What about putting a call through to UNIT?'

'No way,' he said stubbornly. 'Besides, we can't.'

'Why not?'

'There's a time energy barrier around Cardiff. A kind of dome over the city. No one can get in or out.'

'So this isn't just a random event then? Someone's coordinating it?'

'Looks that way,' he said.

Gwen considered for a moment. 'OK, well, how about I organise a police operation to contain the situation?' Before he could protest, as she knew he would, she said quickly, 'We need manpower on this, Jack. Think of us as… as farmers, and the police as sheep dogs. We whistle and give instructions and they… round up the sheep.' She grimaced at her own analogy.

Jack said, 'I don't know, Gwen.'

'Come on, Jack,' she said, 'you know it makes sense. Most people are in bed now, but in five or six hours they'll be waking up, coming out of their houses, and when that happens we'll be faced with a bigger bloodbath than we've got already. If we've got a chance to stop that happening – *any* chance – we've got to take it.'

He was silent for so long that she thought she'd lost him. Then he said, 'OK. Do it.'

'Speak to you later,' she said. 'Happy hunting.'

She cut the connection and punched in the direct line number to Cardiff's Central Police Headquarters, the one that meant she'd be able to speak to someone in authority without first getting pushed from pillar to post. However, she was greeted by an automated message, which informed her that the connection was currently non-operational and politely suggested she try again later. Sighing, Gwen punched in a couple of other, more general numbers, but was met with the same response.

Huffing in frustration, she said, 'Can you believe this? *All* the lines are jammed.'

'Wonder why that could be,' Rhys remarked drily.

She looked at him, trying to decide what best to do. Finally she said, 'Right, change of plan. Forget the Hub for now. We'll head to the police station on foot.'

Rhys raised his finger to his forehead in a casual salute. 'Whatever you say, boss,' he said.

The man in the gutter was not dead, but he looked as though he'd been mauled by a wild animal. When Ianto turned him over, he saw that his jacket and sweatshirt had been shredded, and that there were deep scratches and bite marks in his back, shoulders and arms. Fortunately, the wounds did not look infected, and although the man had lost some blood he was breathing normally and his heartbeat was strong. As soon as he had completed his examination, Ianto stood up and stepped across to the Passat to check on the woman.

She was cowering in the passenger seat, and when Ianto leaned forward to peer in at her through the window, she let out a shrill, breathy scream. What most alarmed him, however, was not how terrified she was, but the fact that she was clearly heavily pregnant.

He held up his hand and smiled. 'Hi,' he said.

The woman just stared at him with wide, shocked eyes.

'I'm here to help,' Ianto said, enunciating the words carefully in the hope that if she couldn't hear him she could at least read his lips. 'Any chance you could unlock this door?'

She didn't respond. Still smiling encouragingly, Ianto said, 'My name's Ianto Jones. What's yours?'

Silence.

Ianto flipped a thumb behind him. 'That man in the gutter. Is he your husband? He's OK, but he needs medical help. You look as though you do too.'

This time the woman *did* react. She sat up straighter in her seat, a look of startled hope on her face. Ianto saw her struggling to push herself upright, to peer around him.

It was clear that she wanted to see the man in the gutter. Ianto stepped back to give her a better view. 'He's OK,' he said again, raising his thumbs to emphasise the fact.

The woman moved carefully across the front seats, holding her belly and wincing as she did so. There was a clunk as she disengaged the central locking system. Ianto pulled the door open.

The woman's face was pale, and sweat had glued her fringe to her forehead. Her eyes darted from left to right.

'Have they gone?' she asked.

'Yes,' said Ianto. 'My friend and I… er, dealt with them.'

The woman looked up at him, her face haunted, disbelieving. 'They were zombies,' she said.

Ianto sighed inwardly. He guessed he was just going to have to go with the flow.

'Yes, they were,' he said, his face deadpan.

'They looked so real. But they can't have been, can they? Zombies don't really exist.'

'No, they don't,' said Ianto.

The woman's eyes flickered past him, to the prone body of her husband. As if afraid of the answer, she whispered, 'What did they do to Trys?'

'He'll be fine,' Ianto assured her. 'Superficial wounds, that's all. So his name's Trys, is it? What's yours?'

'Sarah,' she whispered. 'Er... Sarah Thomas.'

'Nice to meet you, Sarah. I'm Ianto Jones, if you didn't hear me before.' He nodded at her belly. 'I couldn't help noticing... um, when's your baby due?'

Her face creased, as if his question had set off another contraction. Taking deep breaths, she said, 'Any minute, I reckon.'

'Oh, hell,' Ianto said.

Five minutes later, after Sarah had panted her way through her latest contraction, with Ianto offering what little support he could, the Thomases were safely installed in the roomy rear seats of the SUV. Ianto had grabbed a couple of picnic blankets from the boot and handed one to Sarah ('For... er... accidents,' he had muttered). Then he had draped the other across the seat next to her. It had been an effort hauling Trys's dead weight across the pavement and into the big black vehicle and, by the time he had managed it, Ianto was exhausted and covered in blood.

Another suit trashed, he thought ruefully, as he

walked around to the front of the SUV and climbed into the passenger seat. Turning round, he said, 'As soon as my friend, Jack, gets back, we'll take you to the hospital.'

'Will he be long?' asked Sarah anxiously.

'No, he'll be back any minute. Don't worry, everything will be fine.'

As if on cue, Jack's voice suddenly burst from the comms unit attached to his ear.

'*Ianto, help!*'

'Jack!' Ianto shouted. 'Jack, what's wrong? Speak to me!'

There was no answer.

Ianto shoved the door open. 'My friend's in trouble,' he said. 'I've got to go.'

Sarah looked at him incredulously. 'You can't leave me! Not now!'

'I've got to,' Ianto told her miserably. 'I won't be long, I promise.'

'But the contractions are only about a minute apart. I could give birth any second.'

Ianto looked at her in anguish. 'I'm sorry,' he said. 'Look, just… just breathe through the pain and I'll be back before you know it. I'll lock the door. You'll be perfectly safe in here. Nothing can get in.'

He jumped down onto the wet pavement, cutting off Sarah's cries of protest.

Drawing his gun, he ran towards the building site.

EIGHT

'So what happens now?' asked Nina.

St Helen's Hospital was in lockdown, all entrances and exits to the building firmly sealed. No one could get in or out. The dozens, perhaps hundreds, of walking dead that Rianne and Nina had witnessed attack and kill the man in the car park were surrounding the hospital, staring in through the building's glass frontage at the people inside.

At first there had been panic. Lots of people screaming and running. Demanding answers. Demanding action. The staff, who were terrified too, had done their utmost to calm the rising hysteria, to bring the situation under control.

Now there was a sort of uneasy calm. People were still edgy, still scared; some were weeping; a number had been sedated. There had been an attempt to clear the Reception area, to seal it off and evacuate everyone to the upper levels. But perversely the majority of people had refused to leave. The general consensus was that they wanted to *know* what was going on. They wanted to be able to *see* the enemy, to keep tabs on what they were doing.

And, though few people would have admitted it, there was a sense of morbid fascination involved too. Many of the creatures looked awful, terrifying – rotting and scabrous, some with parts of their bodies or their faces missing – but the majority of the tense and muttering multitude which had gathered in Reception simply couldn't stop staring at them, couldn't stop gazing with wonder and awe and disgust at the grotesque and the impossible.

After the initial flurry of panic, things had started to settle down. Despite the tension and the fear, a sort of siege mentality had set in, a touch of the Dunkirk spirit. The people inside the hospital, the *living*, were pulling together, helping one another. The staff were even handing out refreshments, nurses going round with trays of tea and biscuits. Of course, if the walking dead actually *did* something rather than simply stand and stare – if they tried to smash their way into the hospital, for instance – then the situation would undoubtedly change; the screaming and the panic would start all over again. But for now there was a stand-off. Not a truce, as such, but a stillness, a silence. A sense of dreadful anticipation.

Like most people, Rianne and Nina had been drawn to

the Reception area, had felt a peculiar need to be close to the action – or at least close enough to be able to see first-hand what was going on. And, also like most people, they were now staring with fascination and revulsion at the walking corpses – the *zombies* – standing in silent rows outside the hospital. Like sentinels. Like guard dogs.

Rianne shook her head in response to Nina's murmured question. 'I don't know,' she said.

Speaking in a hushed voice, as though afraid the creatures outside might somehow overhear her, Nina said, 'It's almost as if they're waiting.'

Rianne looked at the girl. 'Waiting for what?' she said.

Nina looked back at her with haunted eyes. She gave a little shrug. 'For the order to attack, maybe?'

Gun in one hand, PDA in the other, Ianto ran through the building site, taking care not to slip in the mud and rubble. Eschewing subtlety, he yelled his friend's name as he ran, his eyes darting every which way, constantly on the lookout for movement between the silent, hulking machines, and in and around the roofless shells of houses caged by scaffolding.

Jack's comms were down, which did not bode well. But at least his life-sign readings were still registering on the PDA. Trouble was, they were too imprecise for Ianto to get a fix on Jack's exact location. Jack could be in any one of the two dozen or so soon-to-be 'desirable luxury dwellings' springing up from the few acres of quagmire that Ianto was currently wading through.

In the centre of the site, Ianto stopped and pivoted on his heels, taking a good look round. There were no street lamps here and the half-finished buildings were nothing but featureless blocks of darkness around him, cutting off what little light had previously bled through from the adjacent street. Ianto wished he had a third hand with which he could hold a torch, and thought that maybe he ought to think about rustling up some kind of head-mounted devices for them all. However, the thought of how horrified Jack would be if it was suggested he wear something practical rather than stylish almost made him smile.

'Jack!' he shouted again, his voice bouncing off the black walls around him. 'Jack! Jack!'

This time he received a reply. Jack's voice was tight, as if he was trying to speak and lift weights at the same time.

'Ianto,' he grunted. 'In here.'

Ianto spun round. It was impossible to tell where the voice was coming from. 'I hear you, Jack, but I can't tell where you are. Keep shouting.'

He followed Jack's strained cries towards a house on his left. He squelched across what would one day be an immaculate front lawn and into a rectangular gap awaiting a door. The blackness swallowed him as soon as he stepped into the building, and he shivered as if the new plaster was giving off a clammy chill.

'Jack!' Ianto's voice echoed around him. 'Where are you?'

'In… here…' Jack gasped, so close that Ianto felt as though he could almost have reached out and touched him.

He felt his way along the narrow passage until he came to an opening. He slipped through it, gun arm swinging from left to right.

At first he thought the room was empty, and then, from over by the far wall, there came a scuff and a grunting snarl. Ianto screwed up his eyes and glimpsed what appeared to be a suggestion of movement.

'Jack,' he said cautiously. 'Is that you?'

Jack's voice was a grunt in the darkness. 'Get… her… off me.'

Ianto stepped closer, still pointing his gun. He saw a blue glint on the floor, and realised it was Jack's earpiece, which must have fallen or been pulled off. The PDA cast a metre or so of cold, bluish light before it. Six strides brought Ianto close enough to see Jack lying on his back, trying to hold off the dead teenage girl, who was writhing like a wildcat, her teeth clacking together as she snapped at his face.

Jack glanced up at Ianto with an almost embarrassed expression. 'She's a lot… stronger than… she looks,' he said. The girl snapped at him again. He turned his face aside. 'And her breath really stinks.'

Ianto put his gun away, placed the PDA on the floor, and produced a choke-loop, which the Torchwood team sometimes used on Weevils, from the inside of his jacket. He tried to loop it over the girl's head, and had to snatch his hand back when she twisted in Jack's grasp and snapped at him.

'Hold her still,' he said tetchily.

'I'm… trying,' Jack replied, indignant.

Ianto had another go at snaring the girl, and again almost lost several fingers for his troubles. Sighing, he delved into the left hip pocket of his jacket and produced a nebuliser. This time when the girl twisted her head towards him, he sprayed her full in the face.

He wasn't sure whether the chemicals would have the same immobilising effect on the girl as they did on Weevils – presumably she had no working respiratory system – but it certainly seemed to disorientate her long enough for Ianto to slip the choke-loop over her head. Once that was done, it was only a matter of minutes before he and Jack had the girl gagged and bound. They carried her, still struggling wildly, out of the house, back through the building site, and out onto the street, where the SUV was parked and waiting for them.

In the ten minutes or so that Ianto had been away, three more zombies had arrived, and were now clustered around the SUV, batting ineffectually at the toughened glass of the windows, trying to gain access to the juicy titbits inside.

Jack and Ianto put the trussed and wriggling girl down on the road, and Jack pulled out his gun.

'Oh, you guys are so damn *tiresome*,' he shouted, and ran towards them.

***

116

Andy gave Dawn another worried look as he turned into the road leading to St Helen's Hospital. She looked awful – pale and sweating, her eyes ringed with dark circles. The tea towel around her injured hand was stained red, but the blood loss wasn't *so* great that she would be in any immediate danger.

He thought of what she had said after she'd been bitten, of how she'd been afraid that the suspect might have infected her. But what kind of infection attacked its host so quickly? This was more like the effects of snake venom or something.

Unless…

Andy swallowed, hardly daring to contemplate the possibility.

Unless this was some sort of *alien* infection. A plague from beyond the stars. Some bloody germ or other that turned people into flesh-eating monsters.

He went cold at the prospect. Best to put it out of his head for now, concentrate on the matter in hand.

'Soon be there,' he said, wincing inwardly at the tremor beneath the false cheeriness of his voice.

Whether Dawn could hear him or not he didn't know. A few minutes ago she had closed her eyes, murmuring that she was 'so tired'. Since then he hadn't heard a peep out of her.

'Dawn?' Andy said, hoping that she was just dozing, that she hadn't slipped into a coma. 'Dawn, are you – *Oh, Christ!*'

It was what his headlights had revealed as he had

turned into the hospital car park that had prompted his outburst.

Zombies. Hundreds of the buggers. Forming a cordon around the hospital. Just standing there in ordered rows like… like bloody soldiers or something.

Andy shivered. What were they doing? Massing to attack? Waiting to beam up to the mothership? Or was this some kind of war of attrition? Were the creatures going to wait until the people inside became hungry or desperate enough to take a chance at confronting them, trying to break through their massed ranks?

Whatever the reason, one thing was certain: Andy was not going to get any medical help for Dawn here. He reached for the gear lever, intending to put the car into reverse – and something slammed into the driver's window mere centimetres from his head, making him jump out of his skin.

His head snapped round. A hand, the fingernails purple-black and peeling away, the skin like old green leather, was pressed against the glass. The owner of the hand bent down to peer in at him, and suddenly Andy found himself face to face with a Halloween mask come to life. The flesh of the cheeks was torn and green, the wounds wriggling with maggots. One eye, a withered orb on a thread of tendon, dangled from the socket; the other stared upwards, the pupil only just visible, as if the creature was trying to gaze into its own rotting skull.

As Andy stared in revulsion at the maggoty face, the car lurched violently. Tearing his gaze away from the monstrosity separated from him by nothing more than a thin sheet of glass, he glanced into his rear-view mirror. Dark, ragged figures were milling at the back of the car, shoving and jolting, as if trying to turn the vehicle over.

Terrified, Andy slammed the car into first and stamped on the accelerator, causing the creatures that had gathered around the vehicle to stagger and reel and fall as he sped away. He bumped down to the next level of the car park and turned right into the entrance, knowing that there was an exit at the far end.

A fat female zombie in a purple dress stepped out of the bushes on his left, right into the path of the car. Andy jerked the wheel and the car screeched past her, clipping her leg and sending her spinning away. Immediately another zombie – a thin man in a stained white lab coat – lurched into view from behind a parked van, hands raised, fingers hooked into talons. Andy clenched his teeth as he hit the man head on. There was an almighty bang and the body was thrown across the bonnet and into the air, disappearing in a mass of whirling arms and legs.

The car skidded and spun. Andy wrenched at the wheel, desperately trying to keep control. For an awful second he thought the vehicle was going to flip over, or at the very least hit a tree or another parked car, but then it steadied itself, enabling Andy to drive out of the upraised exit gate and high-tail it out of there.

999 wasn't working. At first Sophie thought it was just her, that she was shaking so much she kept mis-hitting

the buttons. But after a dozen attempts, following which she was *still* receiving an engaged signal, she was forced to conclude that, for the time being at least, the emergency services were out of her reach.

In light of what had just happened, the pink fascia of her phone, imprinted with green bubble-letters spelling out the words 'Party Grrrl', suddenly struck her as hideously inappropriate. Sophie dropped the phone with a clatter on the formica-topped kitchen table, then she pulled out a chair and slumped into it. Still shaking uncontrollably, she leaned forward, propped her elbows on the table, and lowered her head into her hands. Loudly and lustily, she began to cry.

She still couldn't believe what she had seen less than half an hour ago. Every time she recalled it, trying to focus on the details, her mind veered away like a startled deer. Physically, though, she was still reacting to it; her body was close to going into shock. Her hands and feet were freezing and, if she had happened to look in a mirror at that moment, Sophie would have been alarmed by how deathly pale she was, how blue her lips had become.

She had run all the way home, a distance of two miles, and, by the time she had arrived at the front door of the house she shared with her lodger – a graphic design student called Kate, who Sophie had never *really* developed much of a bond with – her stockinged feet were bleeding and embedded with gravel.

Sophie hadn't even noticed. Even now she didn't feel the pain. She sat at the kitchen table, the sobs tearing out of her, her body heaving with tears. She cried for a long time, and when she was done she felt dizzy, sick and drained. Almost subconsciously she crossed to the kettle and flicked it on, took a mug down from the cupboard and spooned instant coffee into it.

When the coffee was ready she re-took her seat at the kitchen table, stared into space and smoked a cigarette. She lit a second from the butt of the first, drawing the smoke deep into her lungs. Recently she'd been trying to give up, and she'd been doing so well too; she'd got down to three a day. But after what she'd seen tonight, all those things like cutting out smoking and eating healthily and going to the gym suddenly seemed so pointless, like trying to deflect a hurricane with an umbrella. Because sooner or later death would come, whatever you did to try and prevent it. It was an unstoppable force: massive, ruthless and unpredictable. Tonight it had taken Winston and Kirsty, and it had nearly taken her too. And, although she had escaped, she felt as if it had the measure of her now, as if she was living on borrowed time.

Sitting in the kitchen, smoking and drinking coffee, her mind drifting haphazardly from one crazy thought to another, Sophie felt a kind of numbness setting in. It was almost comforting in a way. She wished she could sit here for ever, not thinking about anything, cut off from the world. She had always known the world was cruel and unforgiving, but until tonight she had never realised quite *how* cruel, *how* unforgiving, it could be. But now she *did* know, and she wanted no further part of it. It could go on without her as far as she was concerned. She was happy just sitting here, doing nothing.

It was the creak on the stairs which eventually roused her from her torpor. She raised her head slowly, looking across at the kitchen door, willing it not to open. The last thing she wanted right now was Kate babbling on about what a stressful day she'd had at work. Sophie heard the plod of descending footsteps, and braced herself for the inevitable. Just as she'd feared, the door to the kitchen swung wide.

Kate was there, all right, but not the whole of her. There was just her head, eyes and mouth wide open, as if she'd been caught by surprise. The head was hanging by its hair from the clenched fist of a recently dead Asian man in a dark suit, whose wire-framed spectacles dangled from one blackening ear.

The man growled like a dog confronted by a stranger, his slack and stupid gaze fixing on her. As Sophie rose from her seat, thinking almost wearily, *Oh no, not again*, the zombie opened its hand and Kate's head dropped to the floor with a dull, squishy thump.

With a cry of fury and despair, Sophie snatched up her half-empty coffee mug and hurled it with all her strength. Coffee sprayed in an arc across the kitchen as the mug shattered against the zombie's forehead, opening up a wound which trickled with blackish blood.

The zombie didn't flinch, or even blink, from the impact. It just kept shuffling forward, raising its bloodied hands towards her.

'Why can't you just leave me alone!' Sophie screeched at it. She rounded the table and ran towards the kitchen window.

The window was above the sink, and Sophie had to scramble up onto the draining board to reach it, dislodging crockery and pans, which crashed and clanged on the tiled floor. The window itself was divided into three sections. The main picture window in the middle didn't open, but the two side windows did. Sophie groped for the levered catch halfway up the frame and wrenched it upwards, then stooped to lift the bar at the bottom. Her hand closed around the bar at the precise instant that the zombie's hand closed around her ankle.

Immediately the creature began to tighten its grip, grinding her ankle bones beneath its fingers. Sophie screamed, grabbing the window frame as the zombie tried to wrench her from her perch. Half-turning, still clinging to the frame, she drew back her right leg and pistoned it forward. Her foot slammed into the zombie's face with such force that she heard a loud crack as its jaw broke.

The creature didn't seem to feel any pain as such, but it was certainly knocked off balance by the blow. Releasing her ankle, it staggered and dropped to one knee. It was all Sophie needed to turn back to the window and shove it open. Even as the zombie began to rise sluggishly to its feet behind her, she climbed onto the sill and jumped.

It was only a short drop, onto a patch of grass too tiny to be called a lawn at the back of the house, but it was wet and slippery, and as Sophie landed she felt her right leg slide out from under her. She cried out as her knee twisted, flaring with white-hot pain. Clenching her teeth, she forced herself to stand, and then, barefoot and whimpering with agony, she hobbled away.

'Sorry about the loud bangs, boys and girls,' Jack grinned, opening the back door of the SUV. His eyes alighted on Sarah's belly, but his grin wavered not at all. 'Now *that's* going to make life interesting,' he said.

Sarah was all eyes. She looked at the zombies strewn at Jack's feet like roadkill. 'Are those things dead?' she asked in a small voice.

'As dodos,' said Jack, and slipped his Webley back into its holster.

Sarah eyed the gun as if it was a poisonous snake. 'Who exactly *are* you people?'

'Official zombie exterminators for Cardiff City Council, ma'am,' Jack said glibly. 'I can show you some ID if you like.'

Ianto appeared beside him. His previously immaculate suit was spattered with mud and blood. 'How are you?'

'She's very pregnant,' Jack said, still grinning. 'When you told me we had passengers, Ianto, you neglected to mention that tiny detail.'

Ianto frowned. 'Didn't really have time, did I?' Turning back to Sarah, he asked, 'Have you been OK?'

Sarah's obvious terror at a second zombie attack in the space of twenty minutes manifested itself as anger. 'No,

I've been bloody scared,' she snapped. 'Don't *ever* leave us again.'

Ianto stepped back in surprise. Jack chuckled and raised his eyebrows.

'We won't,' Ianto said. 'How are the contractions?'

As quickly as Sarah's anger had appeared, it was gone. Now she just looked exhausted, both physically and emotionally.

'About the same,' she said, 'which is pretty amazing considering.'

'And how's Trys?'

'He's also the same. I think.'

Jack clapped Ianto on the shoulder. 'I'll leave you to practise your bedside manner while I make our other guest comfortable.'

He walked round to the back of the SUV and opened the boot. After dealing with the zombies, Jack had hurried back across the road and helped Ianto carry the girl across to the SUV. They had laid her face-down on the ground before checking to see whether the Thomases were all right. Now Jack bent down to pick her up.

'Come on, sweetheart,' he said. 'We're taking you somewhere warm and cosy.'

He was concentrating on keeping his hands away from the girl's snapping teeth, and so didn't see the zombie underneath the SUV until it was too late. The creature, a boy of no more than seven years old, shot from the darkness with an animal-like snarl and slashed out at him, its fingernails cutting into his throat.

Jack threw himself backwards, intending to whip out his gun and shoot the boy as soon as he was out of the thing's range. But the road was slippery. Jack's feet shot from under him and his skull hit the concrete with a resounding crack. Vaguely aware of the wetness of his own blood pumping from his throat, Jack managed to croak out one word, 'Ianto', before unconsciousness rushed in and everything went black.

NINE

Deep breaths, Andy told himself. *In and out. That's it… that's it…*

Little by little he forced himself to calm down. He loosened his death-grip on the steering wheel and eased his foot off the accelerator. Twice since leaving the hospital car park, he had almost lost control of the car. How ironic it would be to evade the marauding undead only to plough head first into a lamp post or bus shelter.

Beside him, slumped in the passenger seat, Dawn was now deeply unconscious. For a moment Andy envied her. How nice it would be to sleep through this nightmare, wake up when it was over.

That's if she ever does wake up, a little voice whispered in his head. There was no denying that she now looked desperately ill – her flesh lard-white and clammy-looking; her lips almost purple; her eyes sunk deep in bruised sockets.

Andy's priority remained the same: to get her some medical attention – but from where? What if the zombies had isolated *all* the hospitals? Bearing that in mind, his best bet was probably to head back to the station, get the doc there to take a look at her. It wasn't ideal – the medical equipment there was limited – but at least it was a plan, something to work towards.

Feeling more purposeful, he looked around, trying to work out the quickest route – just as a figure hobbled out from behind a white van parked at the side of the road, and stepped directly into his path.

On the surface, the figure appeared to be an attractive young female, wearing a tight, sparkly top and a short skirt. However, she was in such a state that Andy's first assumption was that she was yet another of the walking dead. Her blonde hair was in ratty disarray and she was limping so badly she was all but dragging her left leg behind her. Andy clenched his jaw, deciding in a split second that he would swerve around her if he could, but that he would not be averse to smashing her out of the way if she left him with no alternative.

Then, in the headlights, he saw her eyes widen, the stark – and very human – look of terror on her face, and suddenly he was stamping on the brakes and twisting the wheel in a desperate attempt to avoid running her down.

Although it happened almost too quickly to think

about, he couldn't help experiencing a weird sense of déjà vu as the car slewed to the left, tyres screeching. The girl flashed by on his right – a pale, almost wraith-like form. The main obstacle directly in front of Andy now, across a pavement edged by a high kerb, was a street-length wall punctuated by a variety of garden gates. He wrenched the wheel to the right, though not quickly enough to prevent the passenger-side wheels scraping against the kerb with enough of an impact to cause his teeth to clash painfully together. For a weird moment the car seemed to *lean* to the right, and then it came to a halt in the middle of the road. The engine stalled, and suddenly the world was eerily silent. Deciding that this was most definitely the most stressful night of his career, if not his life, Andy slumped in his seat and released a long, shuddering breath.

It was like a deadly game of hide-and-seek, Gwen thought – she and Rhys sneaking through the streets of Cardiff, peering around corners, scuttling from one piece of cover to the next. They were trying to get from their previous location south of Butetown up to central police headquarters north of the Millennium Stadium. It was no more than a brisk half-hour's walk on a normal day, but present circumstances had transformed the journey into a major expedition across a treacherous war zone. Zombies were everywhere – disorganised and slow-moving, but potentially lethal due to their sheer numbers. Now and again, Gwen and Rhys happened upon grim reminders of just *how* dangerous the creatures could be. So far they had found four partially eaten bodies and one eviscerated dog.

Seeing the first body lying in the street, its guts strewn about like litter, Rhys had thrown up – and then had immediately apologised for being a wuss.

'There's nothing wrong with puking, Rhys. It just shows you're human,' Gwen assured him.

'That's not what you say when I've got my head in the bog the morning after I've had a skinful,' he joked weakly.

They had managed to make it across the River Taff and along Penarth Road, heading towards St Mary Street without serious mishap. However, when Gwen rounded a corner not far from Callaghan Square, she immediately jumped back into the shadows.

Rhys was behind her, gripping his golf club. 'What is it?' he hissed.

'Zombies. Lots of them.'

'Let's have a look.'

'A quick one then. But be careful.'

He raised an eyebrow. 'I'm hardly going to jump out and wave to them, am I?'

Gwen smiled an apology. She was aware she was often overprotective of Rhys, even treated him like a child on occasion, but that was only because he hadn't had the same number of life-threatening experiences as she had, and was therefore more likely to make mistakes. She flattened herself against the wall as he edged past her and peered around the corner. He ducked back again after a few seconds.

'How we gonna get past that lot?' he said.

Before Gwen could respond, there was the tinkling crash of glass, followed instantly by a scream – though of fear rather than agony.

Instantly she was up on her toes. 'There must be people in that café. We've got to help them.'

'How?' asked Rhys.

Gwen peeked around the corner again. Perhaps the sheer number of zombies milling around the café entrance should have alerted her to the fact that there were people inside, but she hadn't been able to see beyond the crush of shuffling bodies. Even the lights of the largely glass-fronted café were off, which she realised either meant they had been damaged whilst the undead had been seeking a way into the building, or they had been deliberately extinguished by the café's occupants in the hope of fooling the creatures into thinking the place was empty. 'Maybe we can get in round the back.'

Rhys looked doubtful. 'If we can get *in*, what's to stop the people in there getting *out*?'

She looked at him, unable to answer, but knowing that she couldn't just walk away from this, that she had to help in whichever way she could. In the end she simply shrugged. 'I don't know, Rhys. But let's have a look, shall we? I mean, anything we can do…'

He nodded resignedly, and she realised that he felt the same way. 'Come on then.'

On an impulse she grabbed the lapels of his jacket and kissed him hard on the lips.

'What's that then?' he asked. 'Last kiss before going into battle?'

She shuddered. 'Don't say "last". Don't even think it.' She took another quick look around the corner, assessing the lie of the land.

'I'll go first,' she said. 'I'll turn sharp left and head for that red Citroën. Soon as I get there, you follow me. I'll cover you in case you get spotted, but keep alert, Rhys. Don't let them catch you by surprise.'

He nodded, and she kissed him briefly again. 'I love you,' she said.

'Love you too,' he said. 'Good luck.'

Gwen took another glance at the zombies, all of which still seemed to be focused on the café, then slipped around the corner like a shadow and ran in a half-crouch to the Citroën she had pointed out to Rhys. As soon as she had dropped out of sight behind the vehicle, Rhys followed her. Behind him there was another crash of glass, another scream. Then he heard a man shout, 'Get back!' Next second he was dropping down on to his haunches beside Gwen.

'They're getting in,' she said. 'We'll have to hurry.' She pointed to her left. 'Bus shelter next, OK? Same procedure as before.'

Again, Rhys gave a brief nod, and Gwen was off, silent and fleet-footed. In this way, moving swiftly but carefully from one bit of cover to the next, they circled around the thirty or so zombies clustered around the front of the café, and round to the alley at the back of the row of shops.

The alley was narrow, little more than a badly lit aisle, barely wide enough for a single car. It was flanked on both sides by the back entrances to parallel rows of retail units. Here were the emergency exits, the tradesmen's entrances, the discarded boxes and the industrial steel bins stinking of rubbish. It was an area of dark shadows and potential hiding places.

'We'll be like sitting ducks in here,' Rhys hissed, sneaking into the alley behind Gwen.

'The sooner we get this done the better, then,' Gwen replied.

Their shadows shrank and lengthened as they moved from one caged orange light to the next. Rhys gripped his golf club in both hands, head turning from left to right, heart constantly lurching as his overactive imagination showed him zombies everywhere – watching from windows, standing in alcoves, emerging from dark places where the light couldn't reach. In front of him, Gwen was swinging her gun from side to side, pointing it into every potential hiding place. They could still hear the commotion from the street – the wordless moans of the undead, the dull thumps and bangs as they tried to gain access to the café, the occasional shouts of the people inside. The sounds were faint at first, but became gradually louder as Gwen and Rhys crept further along the alley. This at least helped them to identify which

133

building they were aiming for. From the back they all looked the same.

When they were a couple of metres from the arch in the high brick wall which led into the café's backyard, Gwen halted and raised a hand.

'What is it?' hissed Rhys.

'I thought I saw something move.'

'What sort of something?'

'I don't know. A shadow.' She smiled nervously. 'Course, I may have imagined it.'

Pumpkin-orange light bathed the wall, but this only made the darkness beyond the arch all the more impenetrable. Indeed, the blackness was so dense that it seemed almost solid. Gwen and Rhys stood motionless on the far side of the alley for a good thirty seconds, both of them holding their breath, their eyes trained on the narrow black entrance. They half-expected something to emerge from it, but nothing did. At last Gwen gestured with her gun and whispered, 'I'm going in.'

She crossed the alley, flattened her back against the wall and edged towards the arch, leading with her gun. Rhys watched, licking his dry lips to moisten them. Gwen was almost at the gap when a white hand snaked over the wall above her and grabbed a fistful of her thick black hair.

She yelled in pain, involuntarily rising onto her toes as the hand tightened into a fist and yanked upwards. Rhys ran across the alley, raised the club and brought it smashing down on the bony wrist. To his surprise there was a howl of pain from the other side of the wall and the hand loosened its grip, allowing Gwen to tear herself free. Without thinking, Rhys ran through the gap in the wall, and into the darkness of the café's backyard, drawing back the golf club for another blow.

The instant he moved out of the light, he knew he'd made a mistake. He blinked wildly, his head jerking as he looked around, but he might as well have been wearing a blindfold. He didn't need to hear Gwen hissing his name in fear and exasperation to know how stupid he'd been. He decided to focus on the patch of blackness where he guessed the owner of the hand must be, and eventually his vision cleared enough for him to be able to make out the long white face of a man cowering in the corner of the yard.

The man was keening like an animal, cradling his injured wrist. In the darkness he resembled a giant spindly insect, all bony knees and elbows. Rhys could smell rotting food from the bins, and now that he was in the yard he realised that someone was banging frantically on what sounded like a metal door over to his left. He sensed movement behind him, and whirled round, heart racing. But it was only Gwen, running across to the place where the thumping was coming from.

'Rhys,' she shouted, 'help me move these bins.'

Rhys peered across the yard at her shadowy figure, and saw what she was doing. She was struggling to move one of two stainless-steel bins, both of which were taller than she was, from in front of a metal fire door. He ran across to help, but as soon as he put his weight behind the bin and started to push, the spindly man struggled to his feet. 'No!' he cried. 'You mustn't!'

Gwen glanced over at the man. 'There's people trapped in there,' she said. 'Can't you hear them? We've got to get them out.'

Upright now, the man stumbled towards them, stretching out his uninjured hand. With his long black coat and thin white face, he looked like a phantom, Rhys thought; like Jacob Marley or something.

'If you let them out, they'll get us,' the spindly man wailed. 'Those dead things. They'll find out we're here.'

Teeth clenched, still struggling with the bin, Gwen muttered, 'If we don't get these people out, those dead things will get *them*.'

The man was shaking his head in frustration. Long stringy hair flapped around his face like rat's tails. 'But don't you see?' he whined in frustration. 'That's what's *meant* to happen. If the dead things get *them*, they won't get *us*. That's my *plan*.'

Rhys scowled, suddenly realising what the man was saying. 'You mean *you* put these bins here? To stop these people getting out?'

The man tilted his head to one side. Rhys wasn't sure in the gloom, but he thought the man was baring his teeth in a wheedling smile.

'Survival of the fittest,' he whined. 'Law of the jungle. Dog eat dog.'

Gwen's voice was low and dangerous. Rhys glanced at her and realised she was pointing her gun at the man.

'You sit down and shut up,' she muttered, 'or I swear to God I'll shoot you here and now.'

For a moment the man remained where he was, hand still outstretched, as though stunned into immobility. Then his arm dropped limply to his side and he crawled away into the corner, curling himself into a ball like a wounded animal.

Panting and sweating, Gwen and Rhys renewed their struggle with the bins. To Rhys it seemed to take an eternity to shift each one even a few centimetres. Throughout that time the pounding on the blocked door became increasingly frantic. A girl, clearly close to hysteria, screamed, 'Oh my God, Martin, get it open! *Get it open!*'

They heard a man snap back at her, his own fear making him angry. 'I'm bloody trying, aren't I? It's locked or jammed or something.'

Still heaving at the bins, Gwen glanced at Rhys, anguish in her eyes, and paused just long enough to shout, 'You in there, listen to me. There's something blocking the door, but we'll have you out in a minute. Try and stay calm.'

'We haven't *got* a minute,' the man yelled back, as if it was Gwen's fault.

'Oh God, hurry up, *hurry up!*' the girl screamed.

Gwen and Rhys attacked the bins with fresh impetus, Gwen's own yells of frustration and rage mingling with the terrified pleas of the girl. Agonisingly slowly, they managed to shift one of the bins far enough away from the door and turned their attention to the second. They had moved it no more than a couple of centimetres, their hands slithering and squeaking on the cold, wet metal, when the girl suddenly screeched, '*Oh God, they're here!*'

'*Let us out! Let us out!*' bellowed the man. His voice was raw and ragged, an animal-like scream of absolute, primal terror. There was a new and frenzied flurry of blows and kicks to the door as sheer panic overwhelmed the couple trapped inside the building. The door banged open, forcing Gwen to jump back. But it opened only a couple of centimetres before hitting the side of the second bin with a resounding clang.

Gwen looked down and saw fingers curling around the door frame as if in the desperate hope of dragging the rest of the body through the impossibly narrow gap. She hurled herself at the bin again, sobbing and swearing with frustration, straining every sinew, willing the damn thing to move. But, even with Rhys's help, the bin seemed to be stuck, its castors embedded in the muddy, cracked concrete of the yard.

And then in a broken, tearful voice, a voice too full of terror to raise itself to little more than a wheezing croak, they heard the girl say, 'Oh God, no… please, no…'

Next moment the *real* screaming began. High and terrible. Screams of unimaginable, unendurable agony. Rhys reeled away, eyes squeezed shut, hands clamped to his ears, his only instinct being to blot out the unbearable sounds from the other side of the door.

Gwen roared, '*No!*' and flew at the bin as if it was an opponent, punching and pounding, tears streaming down her face, teeth bared and eyes wild. When she felt a hand on her arm, she lashed out, missing Rhys's nose by a whisker. His face was bleach-white and slack with shock, his eyes haunted.

'Come on, love,' he said softly. 'Come on, it's over.'

She gaped at him in disbelief and despair, and then she fell into his arms, sobbing and shaking. She had seen death before, of course, many times, but this was so visceral and immediate, so full of terror and agony, that it made her think of Tosh and Owen all over again, made her think of Tosh's life ebbing away right in front of her, and of how utterly useless she had felt, unable to do a thing to prevent it happening.

The screaming finally stopped, and all Gwen and Rhys could hear from inside the building now were the sounds of feeding and the idiot moans of the zombies.

The door banged open and shut, open and shut against the bin. Rotting, worm-like fingers wriggled and writhed in the gap. Seeing them, Gwen bared her teeth in a snarl, broke away from Rhys's embrace and hurled herself at the door. It slammed into place like a guillotine, severing a dozen or so zombie fingers, which pattered to the ground like Saturday night chips dropped by a drunk.

It was a hollow victory. The creatures in there felt no pain, no fear. She whirled away – and her eyes fell on the spindly old man squatting in the corner of the yard, trying to melt into the shadows. Sudden rage overwhelmed her, and she stalked across the yard, drawing her gun, deaf to Rhys's attempts to placate her.

She walked right up to the man and pointed the gun at his face. He whimpered, raising his arms as a flimsy shield.

'You murdered those people,' she muttered, her voice low and wavering, full of revulsion. 'They died in agony because of you. I ought to blow your brains out.'

'Please,' the man whispered, 'please.'

'Gwen,' said Rhys calmly, 'put the gun away. You don't really want to do this. You'd never live with yourself if you pulled that trigger.'

'Oh, I *do* want to do it,' Gwen said. 'Believe me, I do.' Five seconds passed. Then she put the gun away. 'But I'm not going to,' she said. 'Because you're not worth the anguish that Rhys will go through, trying to come to terms with a wife who can shoot someone in cold blood.'

She shuddered, as though shaking off something cold and clammy, and then she said, 'Let's go, Rhys.'

He nodded, slipping an arm around her shoulder as they walked towards the gap in the wall.

Behind them the old man wailed, 'What about me?'

Gwen looked about to retort, but Rhys held up a hand. He walked back to the old man.

'If I were you, mate,' he said acidly, 'I'd find somewhere to hide, and I'd pray that lot in there don't sniff you out. I won't say good luck because I don't wish you any.'

Without another word he turned and walked away.

TEN

Jack sat up with a cry on his lips, and immediately began gulping at the air, with the intention of filling his lungs, re-oxygenating his blood.

He still didn't really understand the physical mechanics of his condition. What *seemed* to happen was that his just-deceased body was held in stasis while time ran backwards over it, repairing wounds and mending broken bones.

Then he became aware that his throat was hurting – *really* stinging, in fact – and that he had the mother of all headaches. *That* wasn't supposed to happen. He brought a hand up to his throat, and found some partly scabbed-over gouges there, and some *very* painful bruising. He cried out as his fingers prodded the tender areas, then sank back onto the bed, feeling dizzy. He realised straight away what had happened. He hadn't died. That zombie kid had opened his throat, and he had lost some blood, but the injuries hadn't been fatal. The long and the short of it was, Jack had simply slipped and knocked himself out.

How *embarrassing*, Jack thought. And how inconvenient. Sometimes it was better to die than not. At least when he died, the time-forces did their stuff, making him good as new, leaving him with no wounds, no scars, no pain. But injuries were merely injuries. They took time to heal. And what was more they bloody *hurt*.

Suddenly aware that he was wet and sticky, Jack looked down to see that the front of his shirt was soaked in congealing blood. He grimaced. 'Oh, gross,' he said.

He looked around, wincing at the throbbing pain in his head. He was back in the Hub, lying on the table in the Autopsy Room. Home sweet home. He wondered how long he'd been out for.

Next second he scrambled to his feet, hand moving instinctively to his gun, as someone screamed.

It was a woman. Gwen? Rising above the pain of his injuries, as he had had to do on so many previous occasions, he ran up the steps and into the main Hub area, his eyes sweeping across the gantries and walkways, the workstations with their glowing computer screens and cluttered glass table tops, the metal tower in the centre constantly streaming with water. There was no one. Or at least no one that he could see. The scream had been brief, but ratcheting, full of pain.

'Gwen?' he shouted, his voice echoing back off the brick walls. 'Ianto?'

'In here, Jack,' Ianto shouted from somewhere below him. He sounded stressed.

'Where's here?' Jack called back.

'Boardroom.'

The Boardroom was in the depths of the Hub, at the end of a corridor that had been converted from a vast pipe, which Jack suspected, from the faint but lingering odour, might once have been one of Cardiff's major sewer outlets. He ran down there, feet clanging on the metal walkways, his speed increasing as another scream came tearing up from below. What the hell was Ianto *doing* down there? Torturing someone?

It was only when he burst into the room, gun at the ready, that his still somewhat fractured memories snapped back into place. Ianto, in his shirtsleeves, hands encased in blood-smeared surgical gloves, eyed the Webley disapprovingly.

'I don't think you're going to need *that*,' he said.

Sarah Thomas, the pregnant woman they had rescued earlier, was lying on a mattress which had been placed on the long, glass-topped table in the Boardroom. Pillows had been bunched behind her back and head, allowing her to half sit up. Her hair was drenched in sweat and her red face was contorted in pain. Jack looked down and saw that she was in the latter stages of giving birth. The mattress was covered in blood and he could see the top of the baby's head.

'My, you *have* been busy,' he remarked, putting his gun away. Then he realised what Sarah was lying on. 'Hey, is that *my* mattress?'

Ianto scowled at him. 'Shut up, Jack, and give me a hand here.'

Jack grinned and said to Sarah, 'I love it when he's masterful.'

Sarah just rolled her eyes, clearly not in the mood for frivolity.

Abruptly becoming serious, Jack said, 'You look as though you're doing a brilliant job here. Both of you.'

Ianto flashed him a brief smile and said, 'You ready for another push, Sarah?'

Sarah inhaled and exhaled rapidly through her mouth, and nodded.

'Whenever you're ready,' Ianto said.

Sarah opened her mouth, screamed and pushed. The baby's head, dark hair plastered to its scalp, bulged between her legs and then slipped back again.

'Again,' Ianto said gently. 'Come on, Sarah, you're nearly there.'

She tried again. And again. Finally, after ten minutes of exhausting effort, the little body, purpley-blue and smeared in blood and vernix, suddenly slithered out from between her legs, trailing the thick blue rope of its umbilical cord. Jack caught the baby as it emerged, gently cradling its tiny head. Ianto, clutching Sarah's hand, laughed with sheer joy. Sarah slumped back onto the pillows in relief and exhaustion.

'It's a boy,' Jack said softly, and grinned. 'Well done.'

He leaned forward and kissed Sarah's cheek. Ianto kissed the other.

Sarah lifted her head. She looked utterly drained, yet suddenly radiant. 'Is he all right?' she asked.

'He's beautiful,' said Jack, 'just like his mother.'

'Can I hold him?'

Jack wrapped the baby in one of the clean towels which Ianto had thought to bring down from upstairs and handed the baby to Sarah. His eyes sparkled as he watched mother and baby together for the first time.

'See?' he said to Ianto. 'This is what it's all about. The miracle of life amidst all this death.'

Ianto looked anything but his usual immaculate self, but he was grinning. All at once he noticed the wounds to Jack's throat and said, 'I thought when you died, it was supposed to—'

'I didn't die,' Jack interrupted curtly.

'You didn't? I thought you had. I told Gwen you had. When she phoned.'

'Yeah, well. I didn't.'

There was an almost embarrassed silence, and then Ianto murmured, 'What about the umbilical cord? The baby's, I mean. And the placenta?'

Jack held up his hands. 'I'll handle it. I've delivered babies before.'

'Have you?' said Ianto surprised. 'When?'

'Long story,' said Jack. 'Why don't you put some coffee on? I think we could all do with some.'

145

'Good idea,' Ianto said and started to trudge away. Sarah called his name and he turned back.

'Thanks,' she said. 'For everything. For being here with me.'

He nodded, and though he remained composed he looked absurdly touched. 'You're welcome,' he said, a little choked.

Ten minutes later, Jack, cleaned up and wearing a fresh shirt, joined Ianto as he was pouring the coffee.

'That smells good,' he said.

'How is she?' Ianto asked.

'Mother and baby are doing just fine. You did a great job back there.'

Ianto nodded briefly. He hesitated a second, and then said, 'I was scared though, Jack. What if something had gone wrong?'

'It didn't,' Jack said reassuringly.

'No, but what if it *had*? I wouldn't have known what to do. As it was, Sarah delivered her baby with no pain relief. I wasn't sure what to give her. I didn't know what was safe in her condition.'

Another pause.

'We need a proper medic, Jack. Someone to replace Owen. We need—'

'I'm working on it,' Jack said curtly, and looked around. 'Hey, where's the zombie? And Sarah's husband? What's his name?'

'Trys,' said Ianto. 'I made up a bed for him in the Hothouse. It's nice and quiet in there. I think he'll be OK.

His life signs are good.'

'And let me guess – the zombie's in the cells.'

Ianto nodded. 'I've put her next door to Janet. They'll be making friends by now.'

'Bitching about us, no doubt. You know how girls are when they get together.' He grinned at his own joke, but Ianto still looked sombre.

'Jack,' he said, 'what would have happened out there tonight if I hadn't been there to save you? What if that zombie and its mates had torn you apart and eaten you? How would you have come back from that? How would you come back if your body was totally destroyed?'

For a moment, Jack looked haunted, as if he had often wondered the same thing. Then the familiar grin – the grin that Ianto knew Jack sometimes wore like a mask – appeared, and he shrugged.

'Who knows?' he said, and reached for a mug of coffee. 'Maybe we ought to try it some time.'

'So what do they call you, then?' Andy glanced at the girl in his rear-view mirror.

She stared back at him with shocked panda eyes.

'What?' she said.

'Your name? What's your name?'

'Oh.'

For a moment she was silent, a slight frown wrinkling her forehead, as if she had put the information down, like a set of keys, and couldn't remember where. Then she said, 'Sophie. Sophie Gould.'

'Nice to meet you, Sophie. I'm Andy. And this is my partner, Dawn.'

Sophie's shell-shocked eyes flickered to regard the WPC slumped in the passenger seat. 'What's wrong with her?' she asked dully.

'She got bit by one of those… creatures,' Andy said.

'Is she gonna be all right?'

'Yeah, she'll be fine,' he replied, more confidently than he felt. 'I was going to take her to hospital, but… well, we couldn't get there. So I'm taking her back to the station now. There's a doctor there. He can look her over. He can check you out too, if you like.'

Aware that he was beginning to babble, he forced himself to shut up.

Sophie nodded vaguely. 'I'm all right.'

'You look to me as though you've hurt your leg,' said Andy.

'What? Oh yeah,' Sophie replied, as if only just realising that her knee was red and swollen.

'So what happened?'

'I twisted it jumping out of a window.'

'Stuntwoman, are you?'

'What?'

'Never mind,' said Andy. 'It was a joke. Not a very good one.'

A short silence fell between them. Andy was driving slowly, keeping his eyes peeled for marauding zombies. Whenever he spotted one, or a group of them, he would extinguish his headlights, change down to second gear and crawl past, in the hope that the creatures would ignore the car.

So far the tactic had worked, and the journey since he had picked up Sophie had been relatively uneventful. The only potentially risky moment had come when a zombie had wandered into the road, right in front of them. On that occasion, Andy had had to stop the car, and he and Sophie had waited, holding their breath, until the creature – a hulking ginger-haired man in a blood-streaked leather jacket – had crossed the road in front of them and ambled away.

'So what's your story?' he asked now, glancing at Sophie again.

At first he thought she wasn't going to answer, and then she haltingly started to tell him what had happened to her that night, the terrible things she'd seen. Finally her voice cracked and she began to sob, lowering her face into her cupped hands, her shoulders heaving. She sobbed for several minutes and then abruptly she stopped. She wiped her eyes with the backs of her hands, smearing mascara across her face.

'Sorry,' she said bleakly.

'Nothing to apologise for,' Andy said. 'You've been incredibly brave.'

She snorted. 'No, I haven't. I ran away and left my best friend to get torn apart by those… things.'

'There was nothing you could have done. If you'd tried to help, you'd be dead now too.'

She was silent a moment, as though contemplating

this. Then she asked, 'Is this happening all over, or just here in Cardiff?'

'I don't know.'

'And, I mean – *why* is it happening? Is it like… Judgement Day or something?'

'No idea,' said Andy. 'Sorry. I'm as much in the dark as you are. It just started happening, and now I'm trying to deal with it as best I can.'

They drove on, cutting through the centre of the city, bypassing the Millennium Stadium and Cardiff Castle, heading up North Road with Bute Park on their left. They saw the black silhouettes of zombies wandering about in the park like lost drunks, massing around the Roman Fort and the tennis courts.

Finally, on the other side of the road, the imposing façade of Police Headquarters came into view, its myriad windows staring down at them.

'*No*,' Andy breathed.

Sophie leaned forward, between the seats. 'What is it?'

'We'll never get in. Look.'

Sophie looked. The police station was under siege. Zombies were massing around it, stumbling up the steps that led to the main entrance, battering against the building with their hands, or their bodies.

As Andy edged closer, he saw that the building had battened down its hatches. All its doors were firmly closed, and the faces of those who had taken refuge inside were peering out of lighted windows. Looking closer, he saw that a number of bodies were strewn on the ground, though whether they were the bodies of the undead or their victims he couldn't be sure. Certainly one car was simply stationary in the opposite lane, its lights on and doors open, as if the occupants had left in a hurry. Another car – a police car like Andy's own, the word 'Heddlu' clearly visible on the side – had mounted the pavement and destroyed a sapling. This car had dark smears on the mostly white bodywork, but its erstwhile occupants were nowhere in sight.

Sophie made a sudden sound, somewhere between a gasp and a whimper. 'They've seen us,' she squeaked, and then her voice suddenly escalated into panic. 'Get us out of here! *Get us out!*'

Andy didn't argue. It was clear that the station would not be the safe haven he had been hoping for. With no clear thought as to where he was heading, except away from the dead eyes and grasping hands of the dozens of zombies which were now turning towards them, he put his foot down and sped away.

Gwen suddenly stopped and slumped against a wall, as if her legs had given out on her. She covered her face with hands that Rhys saw were shaking badly.

'You all right, love?' he asked. He himself felt scooped-out, empty, after the death of the couple in the café.

Gwen's voice, muffled beneath her hands, was trembling with anger. 'That man, that… that…'

Words failed her then, and when her hands dropped

Rhys saw that her face was twisted in abhorrence and rage.

Abruptly she shrieked, a savage war-cry of a sound, and began to kick and pummel the wall, yelling until her voice gave out.

Rhys looked around anxiously, terrified she would attract undue attention, but he didn't try to stop her. She needed to let it out. Gwen was not the sort of person who could bottle things up.

Eventually she slumped again, her fury spent. Rhys opened his arms.

'Come here,' he said softly.

She tumbled into his embrace, and for a minute or more they just stood there in the drizzle, locked together in misery and anguish and fear and mutual comfort.

At last she took a deep breath and broke away. 'I'm OK now,' she said. 'We should be getting on.'

Her phone rang. She scooped it from her pocket. 'Jack? Oh, Andy... hi.'

She listened for a moment, and then said, 'Why, what's happened?'

Rhys saw her face change. She breathed out a long, 'Ohh...' of weary despair. Eventually she said, 'Just go home, Andy. Barricade yourself in. There's nothing else you can do.'

She paused, listening to his response, and the grimace she flashed at Rhys spoke volumes. He knew from her expression that Andy was nearing the end of his tether, bending Gwen's ear, probably demanding to know why

Torchwood weren't doing anything about the situation. He felt a flash of anger and held out his hand for the phone, but Gwen shook her head.

'You'll just have to look after her the best you can,' she said. 'You know the score. I can't work miracles, Andy.'

She half-smiled at his response. When she next spoke her voice was softer. 'That's OK... We all are. Look, just get home and keep yourself safe, all right?'

She put the phone back in her pocket.

'Lovelorn Andy giving you a hard time, is he?' said Rhys.

Gwen cocked a reproving eyebrow. 'He's up against it, just like us. But he gave me some useful information, as it happens. Police HQ is overrun with zombies. Sorry, Rhys, but we'll have to change our plans again.'

Rhys groaned and rubbed a hand over his face. 'You mean we've come all this way for nothing? So what do we do now?'

Gwen's expression suggested they were running out of options, but she tried to sound purposeful. 'We'll revert to our original plan – go back to the Hub.'

'And do what? Hide underground and hope it all goes away?'

'What other choice do we have?' she snapped suddenly, and then immediately she raised both hands. 'Sorry, sorry.'

Rhys blew out a long breath.

'No, love, it's me who should be apologising. You've got equipment at the Hub. Computers and that. You might be able to come up with something. It's just the thought of having to retrace our steps through that... that war zone back there.'

'We'll go down Lloyd George Avenue,' Gwen said. 'It's not far.'

'Far enough,' Rhys replied. 'It's a long, straight road without much cover, that is.' He smiled without humour. 'Valley of death.'

'We'll get transport,' Gwen said. 'Something big and solid.'

'From where?' said Rhys.

'Wherever we can find it.'

'Oh, so we're common car thieves, are we now?'

She shrugged. 'Needs must when the devil drives, Rhys.'

Rhys nodded at the pocket where she kept her phone. 'Why don't you try Jack again, see if he can come and pick us up?'

Gwen had called a flustered Ianto twenty minutes earlier, only to be told that he was in the middle of delivering a baby and that Jack was dead again. It had not been a long conversation.

'Jack and Ianto have enough on their hands,' she said. 'Besides, I'm not using them as a taxi service. I do have my pride, you know.'

'Bloody stubborn is what you are,' Rhys said, albeit with the trace of a smile.

'I think you mean independent, don't you?' said Gwen, smiling back at him.

They set off, emerging from the back alleys along which they had been skulking, and starting down the wide, straight expanse of Lloyd George Avenue, which ran parallel with Bute Street, and stretched all the way from Cardiff city centre to Roald Dahl Plass. The modest houses lining both sides of the road, fronted by grass verges, were dark and quiet, and there appeared to be no sign of zombie activity in the immediate vicinity.

Even so, they felt nervous and exposed, and moved as swiftly and silently as they could, their eyes darting everywhere, their hands tightly clutching their respective weapons. The wet road stretching before them was a rusty, glittering brown under the light from the street lamps. To Rhys, their footsteps sounded like little crackling detonations, which he couldn't believe weren't audible for miles around.

They had been walking for only a couple of minutes when Gwen hissed, 'Rhys, over there.'

At first he thought she had spotted a zombie, and tensed, but then realised she was referring to a silver Mitsubishi Shogun parked in front of a house to their left.

They ran across to it. Gwen tried the doors.

'You didn't honestly expect it to be open, did you?' Rhys whispered.

She shrugged. 'You never know.'

She produced something from the pocket of her jacket, a stubby black circular device, like a miniature hubcap. When she placed it on the door of the car it remained there, clinging like a limpet. Lights with no discernible source rippled across its surface.

'What's that, then? One of your alien doodahs?' said Rhys.

'Sort of. It's something Tosh came up with. But it's derived from alien technology, yes.'

There was the sudden chunky sound of locks disengaging.

'Et voilà!' exclaimed Gwen, grinning.

'What the hell do you think you're doing?'

They spun round to see the Shogun's owner framed in the open doorway of the house behind them. He was in his mid-thirties, hair tousled, face unshaven and rumpled with sleep. He was wearing a grey T-shirt stretched over a burgeoning beer belly and baggy black boxer shorts. In his hands he was brandishing a red squeegee mop.

He's just like me, Rhys thought with a horribly embarrassed sense of shame, *and here we are about to nick his pride and joy*.

He held up his hands, though tried not to make it look as though he was wielding his golf club like a weapon, and flashed his teeth in a contrite grin.

'Hello, mate,' he said. 'Listen, this isn't what it looks like.'

'What were you doing with my—' the man said, and then the expression on his face changed from outraged indignation to an open-mouthed, almost comical, gape.

Rhys realised that the car owner was no longer looking at him. He turned his head, stomach clenching with an even more acute sense of embarrassment when he saw that Gwen was pointing her gun at the man.

'Come on, love, there's no need for that,' he said light-heartedly, trying to flash the man a reassuring smile.

'I'm really sorry,' Gwen said, looking as though she meant it, 'but we need your car. It's a matter of life and death.'

'We'll bring it back when we've finished with it,' Rhys promised.

'So if you could just get us the keys,' Gwen said.

The man looked bewildered and scared. Holding up his hands, as though aping Rhys's actions of a few moments before, he nodded mutely and backed stumblingly into his house. Then his eyes widened further and his head jerked to look at something over Gwen's shoulder.

Rhys followed his gaze. 'Oh, crap,' he said.

Eight zombies had appeared from the shadows of the house opposite and were shambling across the road towards them. One was dressed as a clown, its face a repulsive blend of dark rot and white greasepaint; another was an air hostess, her cap perched at a jaunty angle on her wizened, almost hairless head.

Gwen turned and took a shot at one of the zombies, hitting it in the throat. It rocked back on its heels, and then resumed its advance, thin blood streaming from the wound. Turning back to the man she said urgently, 'Go back into your house and lock yourself in.'

'Gwen, we can't leave him,' said Rhys, 'not now the zombies have seen him. You know what they were like at the café when they knew someone was inside. He'll have to come with us.'

Gwen paused and thought for a moment, then said, 'OK. Run inside and get the keys to the car. Be as quick as you can. I'll hold them off till you get back.'

The man hesitated.

'What are you waiting for?' Gwen snapped.

'I've got a wife and daughter,' said the man. 'They're asleep upstairs. I'm not leaving them.'

Gwen swore. The zombies were moving slowly, and it was a wide road, but there would be nowhere near enough time for the man to wake his family and bring them out to the car before the creatures were upon them. Maybe she and Rhys could take them all out, she thought; there were only eight of them, after all.

At that moment at least a dozen more zombies appeared from between two houses on her left and started moving in their direction.

'What's this?' Rhys shouted, head swivelling from one group of zombies to the other. 'Zombie tactics? They've got us in a pincer movement!'

Gwen took another shot at the zombies, hitting one of them in the shoulder, but it was no more than a token gesture. She knew that, no matter how slow the undead were, there was no way she and Rhys would be able to put them all down before they overwhelmed them with sheer numbers. If she and Rhys had been on their own, she would have suggested beating a hasty retreat, but she couldn't face the thought of leaving a young family to the

ORE: 0182   REG: 03/01   TRAN#: 5159
LE   10/12/2009   EMP: 00042

BORDERS.

Returns

Returns of merchandise purchased from a Borders, Borders Express or Waldenbooks retail store will be permitted only if presented in saleable condition accompanied by the original sales receipt or Borders gift receipt within the time periods specified below. Returns accompanied by the original sales receipt must be made within 30 days of purchase and the purchase price will be refunded in the same form as the original purchase. Returns accompanied by the original Borders gift receipt must be made within 60 days of purchase and the purchase price will be refunded in the form of a return gift card.

Exchanges of opened audio books, music, videos, video games, software and electronics will be permitted subject to the same time periods and receipt requirements as above and can be made for the same item only.

Periodicals, newspapers, comic books, food and drink, digital downloads, gift cards, return gift cards, items marked "non-returnable," "final sale" or the like and out-of-print, collectible or pre-owned items cannot be returned or exchanged.

Returns and exchanges to a Borders, Borders Express or Waldenbooks retail store of merchandise purchased from Borders.com may be permitted in certain circumstances. See Borders.com for details.

mercy of the creatures, not after what had happened at the café.

And so she did the only thing she could – she grabbed Rhys and propelled him towards the house.

'Inside!' she shouted. 'We'll fight them from there.'

'Not sure that's a good idea,' he panted, running along beside her. 'Have you seen *Night of the Living Dead*?'

She scowled. 'Have you got any better ideas?'

ELEVEN

'Now, now, Mildred,' Jack said as the zombie snapped at him, missing his fingers by inches, 'don't be rude.'

Ianto, who was standing behind the chair into which the creature had been secured, raised an eyebrow. 'Mildred?'

Jack removed the last of the sensor pads attached to the zombie's forehead, and straightened up. 'Don't you think she *looks* like a Mildred?'

Deadpan, Ianto said, 'I'd say she's more of a Kylie.'

'In *those* shoes? No way!'

The girl might have been small, but she'd been as lively as a Weevil when they had hauled her up from the cells. Between them, Jack and Ianto had eventually managed to strap her into what Jack – and therefore the rest of them – always referred to as the 'interrogation chair'. It had been part of the fixtures and fittings at Torchwood since Emily Holroyd's era in the 1890s, though the thick leather wrist, ankle and neck restraints had been replaced several times in the intervening years.

Jack and Ianto had attached sensor pads to the girl's head to monitor brain activity – if any – and had taken samples of her blood, skin and hair. Finally they had subjected her to a comprehensive body scan, using the Bekaran deep-tissue scanner, a natty little hand-held X-ray device which Owen had been particularly fond of.

Now the results were scrolling across various computer screens arrayed around the girl's snarling, tethered form – and they were making mighty interesting reading.

Jack raised his eyebrows as he scanned the latest findings.

'Well, that decides it,' he said.

'She isn't human?'

'She never was. In fact, she was never anything. She's a construct. She's made of some kind of alien substance which our equipment can't identify. She's ersatz meat.'

'Like Quorn, you mean?' said Ianto.

Jack laughed. 'Zombie flesh as a vegetarian option. Now *there's* a novel idea.'

Ianto frowned. 'So basically what you're saying is, she's a special effect?'

'But one with substance,' said Jack. 'One that can maim and kill.'

Ianto and Jack looked down thoughtfully at the gnashing, snarling creature in its blood-spattered Girls

Aloud T-shirt, straining against its bonds in front of them.

'But where do these things come from?' asked Ianto. 'Who's creating them?'

'That,' said Jack, 'is the question.'

'That's the best I can do,' Andy said, 'though ideally she probably needs a few stitches. Course of antibiotics too, I shouldn't wonder.'

He straightened up, looking down at Dawn, who was lying unconscious on the settee. He had cleaned, disinfected and bandaged her hand, and now all he could do was hope that the infection raging through her system didn't get any worse.

Given tonight's track record, he had half-expected his street to be crawling with zombies when he had turned into it fifteen minutes earlier. But in fact Canton as a whole had been relatively quiet, compared to other parts of the city. The closest zombie to Andy's flat had been an all-but-skeletal old woman with wispy white hair, who had been dragging herself along the pavement on her stomach three streets away.

Even so, Andy had been nervous as he had fumbled for his keys on the drizzle-slick pavement once he and Sophie had carried Dawn the few metres from the car to the mostly lightless apartment block. Even after they had made it inside and shut the door behind them, he had been wary, half-expecting zombies to lurch out at them from every turn of the stairs.

Now, though, finally, he felt able to relax, at least a little. Of course, he was still anxious about Dawn – she looked like death warmed up – but at least, for the time being, they were safe from the marauding undead.

Despite her swollen knee and lacerated feet, Sophie had been a trooper, helping Andy as much as she could, but now she sank into the armchair next to the settee with a groan.

Andy looked at her, and immediately felt guilty for not noticing before how pasty her mascara-streaked face had become. 'You look as though you could do with a cup of tea and some painkillers,' he said.

The trace of a smile flickered on her face. 'I'd rather have a Harvey Wallbanger. But I suppose I'd better keep my wits about me. Just in case…'

Her words hung in the air between them. Andy knew exactly what she was thinking, for the simple reason that he was thinking precisely the same thing. He knew that neither of them wanted to voice the possibility that there might yet be further horrors in store, and that secretly they were both wondering how and when this terrible nightmare would end.

He wondered whether he ought to say something optimistic, reassuring, but nothing that came to mind struck him as anything but hollow. In the end he simply muttered, 'I'll stick the kettle on,' and sloped out of the room, feeling that somehow he had let the side down.

He was using a spoon to alternately prod the teabags in two mugs, watching the boiling water darken to the colour of chestnuts, when Sophie appeared in the kitchen behind him.

'Don't s'pose there's any chance of a hot bath?' she asked.

'Sure, help yourself,' said Andy. 'First door on the left. You'll find clean towels in the airing cupboard. Oh, and you might as well take these with you as you go.' He handed her a pack of Ibuprofen and hastily scooped the tea bag out of her mug before splashing milk into it. 'Sugar?'

'I'm sweet enough, thanks,' she said with weary humour, and limped out of the room.

Andy heard her enter the bathroom and close the door. A moment later came the soft, somehow comforting spatter of water on plastic. He took a long sip of his tea and closed his eyes, relishing the momentary stillness. He felt utterly exhausted, and yet at the same time he couldn't imagine sleeping ever again – not while zombies were still roaming the streets of Cardiff, at any rate.

When he'd finished his tea, he plodded through to the hallway and tapped on the bathroom door. 'Would you like me to find you some clean clothes to change into?' he asked.

He heard the gentle lap of water. 'Don't suppose you've got a nice cocktail dress I can wear?' she replied.

Andy surprised himself by laughing. 'Mine's in the wash, sorry. T-shirt and jeans do you?'

'Guess it'll have to,' she replied. He could tell from her voice that she was smiling.

He selected a red T-shirt and his tightest black jeans from the drawers in his bedroom, and knocked on the bathroom door again. 'I'll leave the clothes outside,' he told her. 'You might have to roll the jeans up a bit.'

She didn't reply. And then he heard a small sound – something like a sob.

'Sophie?' he said. 'You OK?'

Another pause. Then in a cracked voice she said, 'Yeah.'

'You sure?'

This time her response was more decisive, as if she was really making an effort. 'Yeah, I'm fine. Honestly. I'm… I'll be OK.'

'Right,' he said. 'Well, listen, you just… just relax, all right? Take your time. And when you're ready I'll make us a bite to eat. Cheese on toast or something. Sound OK?'

'Sounds great,' she said.

'Right then,' said Andy. He started to move away.

'Andy?' she said.

He paused. 'Yeah.'

'Thanks. For everything, I mean. For saving my life.'

'You're welcome,' he said.

He went into the kitchen and busied himself slicing cheese and tomatoes for their post-midnight snack. He was lifting a couple of plates down from the overhead cupboard when he heard padding footsteps behind him.

'Hope you don't mind your cheddar extra mature,' he said, glancing over his shoulder.

But it wasn't Sophie who had entered the kitchen; it was Dawn.

She was glaring at him, though her eyes were glazed and dead. A string of drool was hanging from her lips, which were curled back from her teeth. She raised her hands – one bandaged, one not – and hooked her fingers into claws, like a child playing at witches. Then, from down in her throat, she began to growl, low and threatening, like a dog.

I really don't need this, Andy thought with a kind of weary irritability, and snatched the cheese knife from the counter beside him. Holding it up, he warned, 'Keep back.' Then he realised what he was doing and decided to try a different tack. 'Dawn!' he said firmly. 'Dawn, can you hear me?'

She shuffled towards him, still snarling and drooling. Andy took another step back, the base of his spine nudging the handle of the cutlery drawer.

'Dawn!' he shouted again. 'Listen to me. It's Andy! We're partners, remember? We're *mates*.'

There was no recognition in her eyes, nothing but a flat, dull hunger.

Maybe he could knock her out, Andy thought, or disable her in some way. Without taking his eyes off her, he put the knife on the counter behind him and reached for the handcuffs on his belt. But then he remembered he had used the cuffs to restrain the zombie at the party earlier that evening. He took a quick glance over his shoulder, looking for something else he could use.

As soon as he broke eye contact with her, she leaped at him.

Unlike most of the other zombies he had encountered, she was fast. Fast and ferocious. Maybe it was because she wasn't actually dead – or was only *just* dead, he couldn't help thinking – but she had crossed the room and was at his throat almost before Andy could react. At the last possible instant he threw up his arms and managed to deflect her clawing hands. She went for him again, but this time he managed to grab her wrists, her forward momentum forcing him back against the kitchen units with enough force to rattle the cutlery in the drawers.

'Dawn!' he shouted again, but she just dipped her head and snapped at his face. Her teeth clacked together, mere millimetres from the tip of his nose. He tried to wrestle her off him, to use his superior height and strength to subdue her, but it was as though her muscles were locked, immovable.

Her feral, chalk-white face filled his vision. Clots of her spittle flecked his face and he could smell her hot, sour breath.

Then Andy glimpsed something above her head, something white, bird-like, swooping down on her. He realised it was a towel only when it settled over her head and was pulled tight across her face, yanking her backwards.

Immediately he realised what had happened. Sophie had entered the kitchen behind Dawn and had thrown a towel – maybe the one she had been using to contain her damp hair – over the other girl's head. She was gripping the towel in both fists now, tugging back on it, trying to pull Dawn off balance.

Andy helped her, hooking his foot around Dawn's ankles and whipping her feet from under her. Towel still wrapped around her face, Dawn fell, Sophie jumping back as quickly as her injured leg would allow as the WPC thumped heavily to the tiled floor.

Like a wrestler going for the fall, Andy dropped unceremoniously onto his partner's body, covering her limbs with his own, using his weight to immobilise her. She bucked and thrashed beneath him, but he held on, pressing her to the ground.

Glancing up at Sophie, he shouted, 'Get me two more towels, quick!'

Sophie limped away, and returned less than a minute later with a couple of fluffy white towels from the airing cupboard in the bathroom.

'Twist them into ropes!' Andy gasped. 'We need to… tie her up.'

Sophie did as he asked, and then dropped to Andy's side, wincing at the flare of pain in her knee. Together the two of them wrapped and tied the towels first around Dawn's hands, and then her feet.

By the time they had done, they were both sweating, Sophie's damp blonde hair sticking to her flushed cheeks.

'What do we… do with her… now?' she panted, looking down at Dawn's writhing form.

'Suppose we'll have to stick her in the bedroom,' Andy said. 'I'll tie something round the handle to stop her getting out.'

He sat back on his haunches and let out a long, heartfelt breath. Then he looked at Sophie and gave her a shaky smile.

'By the way,' he said, 'those jeans really suit you.'

'The windows are the most vulnerable points,' said Gwen. 'Have you got any wood we can cover them with?'

Rhys and the owner of the house, whose name was Keith Samuels, were struggling out of the front room and into the hallway with a heavy sideboard to shove up against the front door. A constant backdrop of dull, meaty thuds accompanied their attempts to make the building secure, and occasionally a window would rattle, causing Gwen's stomach to flip over. So far, though, the zombies didn't seem to have worked out that the windows were the house's weak points.

'Don't think so,' Keith panted.

'It's only in movies where people have window-sized sheets of wood lying about,' said Rhys. 'But then the things they're trying to keep out always seem to come down the chimney anyway.'

'We haven't got a chimney,' Keith said.

'Well, that's something at any rate,' Rhys replied.

Frustrated, Gwen said, 'Haven't you got *anything* we can use?'

Keith thought about it. 'There's a chalkboard in the

kitchen. And Jaz has got a big cork noticeboard on her wall. She sticks photos and things on it.'

'Well, that's a start,' said Gwen, and called down the hallway. 'Jaz, will you get your noticeboard for me?'

Jasmine, aged eleven, a pretty little slip of a thing, had been helping her mum, Naomi, wedge small but heavy items – the toaster, the microwave – into the barricade of furniture against the back door. She looked at Naomi with wide, scared eyes, as if for approval.

Naomi – short and bespectacled, with black spiky hair – pursed her lips but gave a curt nod, and the little girl scampered upstairs.

'What about the kitchen table?' Gwen said. 'That's nice and big. We could break that up.'

'You're *not* breaking up my kitchen table,' Naomi bridled, overhearing her. Ever since being roused from her bed she had been acting as if Gwen and Rhys were responsible for the chaos that had befallen her family, as if the two of them had deliberately brought it along in their wake. 'That was a wedding present from Mam and Dad.'

Gwen took a deep breath and counted to five as she walked the short distance along the hallway to the kitchen at the back of the house. She entered the room, flashing Naomi one of her warmest smiles.

'Well, it's like this, see,' she said sweetly. 'If we don't barricade the house, those things out there – those *dead* things – will get in. And if they get in, they'll rip us apart with their bare hands and they'll eat us. But if you think it's worth risking that happening to your daughter for the sake of an old table…'

She broke off. Tears were sparkling in Naomi's eyes, and suddenly Gwen realised where the woman's hostility was coming from. It was fear. Plain and simple. Naomi Samuels was terrified.

Instinctively Gwen stepped forward and enfolded the other woman in a hug, the way that Rhys did to her when she'd had a bad day.

'Hey, come on,' she said gently. 'Everything'll be all right. But we've got to pull together on this. OK?'

Huddled against Gwen like a child seeking comfort, Naomi nodded.

Sarah Thomas and her baby son were sleeping. Watching them, Jack smiled, but he couldn't help feeling a pang of sadness at the knowledge that, unless his circumstances changed drastically over the next half-century or so, he would outlive this boy. As the years slipped past, he himself would remain unchanged, while this tiny human being, less than an hour old, grew and blossomed, withered and died. Jack had lost so many friends over the years. He had been to so many funerals and cried so many tears that he was now all but cried out. That still didn't stop him feeling each new death as keenly as the last, however. Blowing a kiss to the sleeping mother and child, he turned and slipped silently away.

Upstairs, Ianto was fussing round the 'pod', which had become something of a pet project of his. In light of their recent discovery, he and Jack had earlier spent twenty minutes discussing strategy over mugs of excellent Java Santos, but the only conclusion they had come to was that their new information didn't really add much in a practical sense to what they already knew. OK, so the zombies were not *actually* the newly risen dead of Cardiff, but how did that usefully change things? It still didn't give them any insight into who or what might be responsible for the 'invasion' – and, more especially, why it was taking place. Was the outbreak a random occurrence, perhaps some freakish quirk of the Rift, or was it part of the sinister agenda of an evil mastermind, or even a race of aliens, who were currently lurking somewhere in the shadows, waiting for the right moment to emerge?

In the end, Jack had called a halt to the discussion, saying that they both needed to go away and indulge in a little private 'thinking time'. Now, however, he was back, having thought himself to a standstill.

'Any ideas?' he asked, his voice ringing around the Hub.

Ianto, who had changed into a blue suit, pink shirt and blue flowery tie, straightened from his examination of the pod and shook his head. 'Not a sausage. You?'

'Nada,' Jack admitted. 'What say we just go tearing round the streets, kicking asses and looking for clues?'

'I don't think that's—' Ianto began, and then he looked up, to a point above Jack's head. 'Oh.'

Jack turned, following his gaze. A man was standing on the walkway of the level above them, looking down, swaying slightly from side to side. It was Trys Thomas, and he looked ghastly. His face was fish-belly white, his eyes flecks of grey flint in sunken hollows. He wore a slack expression, as if he was drugged or sleepwalking.

'Hey there!' Jack said, raising a hand. 'How you doin'?'

Trys did not reply. Instead his head swung drunkenly from side to side, as if he was looking for an access point to the floor below. Sure enough, he shuffled to the metal steps like an old man and began to clang down them. Jack moved forward to greet him, but Ianto said, 'Careful, Jack.'

'I'm always careful,' Jack said out of the corner of his mouth. 'Just be ready with the handcuffs.'

'If I had a penny for every time you've used that line,' Ianto deadpanned.

Jack shot him a look, then strolled across to the bottom of the metal stairs, like a one-man welcoming committee for a visiting dignitary.

'Good to see you up and about, Trys,' he said. 'It is Trys, isn't it? Guess you're wondering where the hell you are, huh?'

The blankness of Trys's eyes, and the way he moved his head, made Jack think of a blind man fixing someone's position by the sound of their voice.

'Sure you are,' Jack continued breezily, studying Trys's face for any kind of reaction, any flicker of humanity. 'Well, this is the Hub, I'm Captain Jack Harkness and that there is Ianto Jones. And guess what? Your wife Sarah's downstairs, safe and well. Remember Sarah? Remember how she was all big and fat the last time you saw her? Well, I bet you're just dying to know what's been happening while you've been asleep, huh? Want me to tell you?'

Trys was only a few steps from the bottom of the stairs now. His dead eyes were still fixed on Jack, but it was clear that he had no interest in, or understanding of, Jack's words.

All at once he raised his hands and lunged forward. Ianto shouted a warning, but Jack was ready.

'Oh no, you don't!' he cried, grabbing Trys's hands and stepping back. 'You don't catch me out a second time.'

He continued to move backwards at speed, like a ballroom dancer, swinging his partner after him. Trys was shorter than Jack, and his feet barely touched the floor, the toes of his shoes scuffing the metal. Restrained by Jack's grip, he tried to crane his neck forward, to snap at Jack's face, but Jack evaded him easily.

'Never on a first date,' he said with a good-natured grin, and swept Trys around and across the floor, bypassing the workstations and the zombie he had nicknamed Mildred, which was still strapped in the interrogation chair. Mildred watched them pass with the flat eyes of a snake alert for prey. Jack winked at her and swept Trys across to where Ianto was now waiting, beside a rusty but torso-thick support stanchion, handcuffs at the ready.

The two of them were used to subduing strong and vicious Weevils, and it took them no more than a few seconds to drag Trys's arms behind his back and cuff him to the stanchion. When he was secure, Jack and Ianto stepped away, out of range of his snapping teeth. Trys kept trying to walk towards them, and couldn't seem to work out why he was unable to do so. His constant, frustrated efforts were rather pathetic to see.

'What are we going to tell Sarah?' Ianto said sadly.

Jack looked grim. 'Maybe we won't have to tell her anything.'

Ianto frowned. 'What do you mean?'

'Hey, don't look at me like that! What do you take me for? What I *mean* is that Trys and Mildred are different. She's not a real zombie, so maybe he's not one too.'

'His condition could be psychosomatic, you mean?'

Jack shrugged. 'Let's find out, shall we?'

It was decided, for the sake of convenience, to cuff Mildred to a stanchion on the far side of the Hub for now, and to transfer Trys to the interrogation chair in order to run some tests on him. Jack managed to seal Mildred's mouth with a strip of duct tape without getting his fingers bitten off, and Ianto slipped a choke-loop attached to a metre-long metal pole over her head. Jack then undid the leather straps securing her to the chair and Ianto directed her across the metal floor of the Hub to another support stanchion on the far side of the vast room.

The sound began as a gentle, almost musical warbling. Jack, who was walking beside Ianto with a second set of handcuffs, came to a halt, a puzzled expression on his face.

'You hear that?'

Ianto nodded. 'What is it?'

'I don't know. It's kinda hard to pin down.'

'It seems to be coming from… everywhere,' Ianto said, looking around. 'It sounds like a song.'

Jack frowned. 'Let's worry about one thing at a time. Her first; *then* we'll work out where the music's coming from.'

They started walking again, Ianto using the metal pole to urge the zombie onwards. The warbling sound grew louder. Jack and Ianto looked at each other. Another few steps, and it was becoming less like a song and more like the howling shriek of an alarm.

They halted again, almost in unison. The sound was unearthly, alien. It filled the Hub with echoes, which resounded and clashed, feeding off one another.

Jack looked up into the vast vault of shadows above him, where the pteranodon could sometimes be seen, swooping and circling.

'What the hell *is* that?' he demanded, hands over his ears.

Ianto cast about, looking for an answer. His gaze fell on a nearby workbench.

'Look,' he breathed.

Jack looked. 'My God.'

The partially reconstituted pod was going crazy. Coloured lights were flickering across its surface in rapid, but seemingly haphazard patterns. From deep within it emanated a kind of glow, a pulse, like something alive. Now that Ianto had identified it, it was clear that this was the source of the peculiar alien ululation, the heart-rending sound that was somewhere between symphony, siren and scream.

Ianto looked at Mildred and saw the flickering lights of the pod reflected in her dull, silvery eyes.

'It's her,' he said. 'Jack, it's reacting to her.'

Jack nodded. It was true. Unless it was an almighty coincidence, the pod was responding to the proximity of the false zombie, the ersatz meat.

'*Now* we're getting somewhere,' he muttered.

TWELVE

The ceaseless thumping was setting them all on edge. It was a constant barrage on every wall, door and boarded-up window, a mindless tattoo of heavy-handed thuds, underpinned with the wordless, idiot groaning of the undead.

Naomi was twitchy, clearly close to the end of her tether. All five of them were sitting in the front room, Gwen, Rhys and Keith gamely trying to make conversation, when she suddenly slammed down her coffee mug and shrieked, 'Why don't they just *stop?*'

Jasmine, clutching a yellow rabbit and seeming much younger than her eleven years, abruptly burst into tears.

Gwen and Rhys looked meaningfully at each other, knowing how much more volatile an already terrifying situation could become if panic set in.

Keith said, 'Hey, come on, love,' and tried to put his arms round his wife, only for her to flinch away from him as if he was a stranger.

Gwen leaned forward. 'Naomi,' she said gently, 'Naomi, listen to me. I know how scared you are, and that's understandable. But we have got to stay calm and focused. For the time being, we've just got to sit this out.'

Naomi homed in on her. It was evident she was looking for a target on which to vent her spleen. '*Why?*' she said acidly. '*Why* do we have to stay calm?'

'Because if we start to panic, we lose control. And if we lose control, we make mistakes. And if we make mistakes, then those creatures out there will get us. Believe me, I know.'

Naomi sneered. 'How could you *know?*'

'She's a secret agent or something,' Keith told his wife, a note of admiration in his voice. 'She's got a gun and everything.'

Gwen winced. Jasmine looked at her wide-eyed, as if she expected Gwen to shoot her through the head at any moment. Standing up with a sigh, Gwen said, 'I'll make us all some more coffee.'

She went through to the kitchen, put the kettle on, and – because all the chairs had been used in the barricade – sat on the floor. She rested her forehead on her knees and let out a big sigh, attempting to block out the thuds and thumps around her, to find a quiet, still place into which she could retreat, if only for a few moments.

Suddenly she heard the scuff of a footstep, and her head snapped up. For a split second she thought the zombies had broken in; she expected to see some rotting monstrosity looming over her. Instinctively she reached for her gun – but her hand froze when she saw that it was only Jasmine who had entered the kitchen. The little girl looked down at her curiously.

'Why are you sitting on the floor?'

Gwen smiled. 'Because there aren't any chairs.'

Jasmine accepted the explanation without comment. 'Dad says I can have some milk.'

'OK,' said Gwen. 'Would you like me to warm it up for you?'

Jasmine pulled a face. 'I hate warm milk.'

'Me too,' Gwen said. 'Hot chocolate's nice, though. Warm milk with a couple of spoonfuls of chocolate powder. Lovely.'

Jasmine almost smiled. Nodding at the floppy yellow rabbit, which the girl was still cradling in the crook of her arm, Gwen asked, 'What's his name then?'

'It's a her,' said Jasmine.

'Oh, I *do* beg your pardon,' said Gwen, rolling her eyes and making Jasmine giggle. 'Of course, I should have realised. What's *her* name?'

'Sunny,' said Jasmine. 'Cos she's yellow.'

Gwen nodded. 'Good name.'

She watched Jasmine open the fridge and take out the milk carton, the rabbit still tucked under her arm.

'When I was your age,' Gwen said, 'I had a toy monkey.

Still got her, actually. My gran gave her to me. Her name's Bonzo. The monkey's name, that is, not my gran's.'

Jasmine giggled again. 'Bonzo's a funny name for a girl.'

'Suppose it is, really,' said Gwen. 'But there was a famous gorilla called Bonzo, so I called my monkey after him. Do you want a hand with that?'

Jasmine was struggling with the heavy milk carton, slopping milk on the counter as she tried to pour it. She nodded, so Gwen took the carton and poured the milk for her, then handed Jasmine the mug.

'There you go, sweetheart. Will you do me a favour and tell that thirsty lot in there that the coffee will be ready in one more minute?'

'OK,' Jasmine said.

She trotted off on her errand. Gwen was spooning coffee into four mugs when Rhys said, 'You've got a lovely way with kids, you know.'

Glancing at him over her shoulder, Gwen said, 'Were you eavesdropping, Rhys Williams?'

'No,' said Rhys innocently, 'I just didn't want to interrupt, that's all.'

She raised her eyebrows and went back to making the coffee. Quietly Rhys said, 'You'll make a great mum, you will. One day.'

'Yeah, well…' said Gwen non-committally without looking at him. They had talked about this before, and it remained a prickly subject between them.

'That's if we ever get out of this,' Rhys added.

Now Gwen *did* look at him, and immediately noted the worry etched on his face. She crossed to him and took his hands. 'We will,' she said. 'I promise.'

'But how, love? We're trapped in here,' he said.

Gwen looked at him with utter conviction. 'Jack will come up with something. I know he will.'

No sooner were the words out of her mouth than they both heard the shattering tinkle of glass from the front room. They exchanged a horrified glance and ran down the hallway, almost colliding with the Samuelses, who were coming out of the door.

'They're breaking in,' Keith said simply, looking at Gwen with wide, frightened eyes.

As if to confirm his words, the sound of splintering wood could now clearly be heard.

'Upstairs,' Gwen snapped. Then she drew her gun and stepped into the front room to face the invaders.

'Just as I thought,' Jack said.

'He's not dead?' said Ianto.

'Not only is he not dead, but aside from those superficial wounds on his back, there's absolutely nothing wrong with him. There's no sign of infection, and his life signs are not only normal, they're *strong*. It's almost as though, when Trys was attacked, the zombies passed a kind of… thought-virus on to him. A hypnotic suggestion.'

'They made him *think* he was going to become a zombie, so he *became* a zombie?'

'Exactly!' Jack said.

'And what about you?' asked Ianto.

'What do you mean?'

'You were attacked too. How do I know *you* won't suddenly become one?'

Jack looked at him reprovingly. 'This is *me* you're talking about, Ianto.'

Ianto shrugged. 'The question still stands.'

Dismissively Jack said, 'I'm different. I know these things aren't real, so I'm hardly going to become one, am I? Give me *some* credit.'

'OK,' Ianto said quietly. 'But just in case you *do* become one, can I request permission now, while you're still able to grant it, to shoot you in the head? *Without* incurring a pay cut.'

Jack grinned. 'Permission granted,' he said.

Ianto nodded seriously. 'So,' he said, 'how do we persuade Trys that he isn't a zombie?'

Jack straightened from the readout screen which had been collating Trys's physical data and pointed at the sheets of paper in Ianto's hand. 'Well, I'm kinda hoping you've got the answer right there. That's all the stuff you could find from the night the pod came down?'

Ianto brandished the sheaf of papers in his hand. 'Press coverage, police reports, energy readings…'

'And I'm guessing, from the way you scampered across here like an excited puppy, that you've found something?'

Ianto looked pained. 'I don't "scamper". I stride. Briskly but with dignity.'

'I detected a definite scampering motion,' said Jack.

Ianto tutted and shook his head, and returned his attention to the reports in his hand.

'Are you sulking now?' asked Jack.

'No, I'm not sulking,' Ianto replied. 'I'm collating.'

'So collate me,' Jack said.

Ianto pursed his lips and said, 'As you know, the pod came down in Splott three months ago, killing sixty-three people and causing damage to a number of buildings. It was 3.13 a.m. so most of those buildings – retail establishments, warehouses – were empty at the time, but one was occupied.'

'The cinema, right?' said Jack.

Ianto nodded. 'The Regal Cinema on Railway Street, correct. It's a privately run cinema, which has been owned by the – ahem – Adams family since 1897.' He shot Jack a brief glance.

Jack mimed pulling a zip across his mouth. 'My lips are sealed. Carry on.'

'Perhaps what none of us thought to ask,' continued Ianto, 'was *why* the Regal was occupied at the time.'

Jack shrugged. 'I just assumed there was a private screening.'

'And you'd be right. But of what?'

'Adult movies, maybe?'

'Wrong,' Ianto said. With a flourish he produced a photocopied handbill and passed it to Jack.

Jack looked at the lurid, blood-dripping letters. *The All-Night Zombie Horror Show,*' he murmured. 'Let the walking dead entertain you from dusk till dawn.' His eyes scanned the list of movies, and then he looked up with a grin. 'Good work, Ianto.'

'There's more,' Ianto said. 'Sixty-three people died that night, but there were sixty-four in the cinema. The only survivor was twenty-two-year-old Oscar Phillips, of Madoc Road, Splott.'

'And where's Oscar now?' Jack asked.

'He's in a coma in St Helen's Hospital,' Ianto replied.

THIRTEEN

In a hospital bed, linked up to all manner of drips and monitors, lay an unremarkable man. He was not much to look at – slight, bordering on weedy; plain, bordering on ugly; medium height; sandy hair. He had been lying here for over three months now, still and silent. He was fed through a tube, and he breathed with the aid of a respirator. He was bathed once a day and turned regularly to avoid the onset of bedsores. His mother, Clare, who was fifty-one years old (though she looked older), visited him every morning, and sometimes in the evenings too. She talked to him, and read to him, and played him his favourite music – Queen, Bon Jovi, Bruce Springsteen – in the hope that he might twitch a finger or flicker an eyelid in response. But in three months he had done neither of these things, nor anything else besides.

Oscar Phillips slept on while the world passed him by.

Oscar was alone now, not exactly neglected but temporarily abandoned. Something was happening elsewhere in the hospital, something extraordinary, and the staff were understandably distracted. Which was why, when the wave patterns on the EEG machine monitoring his brain activity began to spike and trough crazily, there was no one there to note it; which was why, when his body began to twitch and shudder, there were no witnesses. Behind his eyelids, Oscar's eyes jerked and rolled, as though he was having a nightmare. His lips, which were greased to stop them from drying out, parted with a tiny pop and he released a low, wordless moan.

Gwen took out half a dozen zombies before realising it was hopeless. It was evident, from those she could see through the gap in the splintered noticeboard nailed across the broken window, that considerably more than the original twenty or so were now massing outside the house. She wondered briefly what had drawn them here – the smell of fresh meat? Some kind of telepathic communication? Whatever it was, they were now breaching the house's meagre defences, driven by the only instinct they knew – the instinct to kill and devour.

Above her, Gwen could hear pounding feet, as Rhys and the Samuelses raced upstairs. She fired off one more round, dropping another zombie in a spatter of blood and brains, and then she set off after them.

'We need somewhere we can defend. An attic or

something,' she shouted as she ran up the stairs.

When she reached the upper landing, Keith was hovering underneath a square wooden panel in the ceiling, whilst behind him Naomi was clutching Jasmine, both of them shaking with fear. Keith looked pale and vaguely startled, like a rabbit caught in the headlights. Gwen recognised the signs, knew that the trauma of the situation had rendered him almost incapable of action.

'Where's Rhys?' she said, looking around.

Keith stared at her blankly.

Exasperated, Gwen said, 'Have you got a ladder, Keith? We need a ladder.'

'It's all right, love, I've got a chair,' Rhys said, emerging from Jasmine's bedroom, pushing a typing chair on castors.

'Rhys, I could snog you,' she exclaimed.

'Save it till later. I'll hold the chair, you climb up.'

From down below came the sound of more wood splintering, and then a crashing thump, followed by what could only be described as a blundering inrush of movement.

They're through, Gwen thought as she leaped on to the chair and raised her hands above her head. She pushed the wooden panel with all her strength, and experienced a brief, panicky moment when she thought it wasn't going to give. Then it popped up so suddenly that she almost lost her balance. She shoved the panel to one side, hauled herself up until her head was poking through the gap and peered into the darkness.

Immediately dust ambushed her, making her sneeze, and sneeze again. The third time she did it, she thought angrily: *I haven't got time for this!* She wiped her streaming nose and eyes with her sleeve and saw that directly in front of her was a folding metal ladder on a hinge. Ignoring the ache in her hip, she scrambled up into the attic, unfolded the ladder and pushed it down through the hole.

'Quickly!' she shouted.

'Women and children first,' said Rhys, all but wrenching Jasmine out of her mother's grasp and plonking her halfway up the ladder. Gwen was afraid the girl would freeze, but Jasmine scuttled up the ladder like a mouse. Naomi followed, Gwen reaching down to grab her hand and haul her up. Then came Keith, with Rhys bringing up the rear.

Rhys was on the bottom rung of the ladder, his face dangerously close to Keith's slippered feet, when Gwen, looking down through the gap, saw the green-black face of a zombie suddenly pop into view halfway up the stairs.

'*Quickly!*' she yelled. '*They're coming!*'

Keith glanced behind him, let out a terrified yelp – and froze.

'Go on, mate,' Rhys shouted behind him. 'What the hell have you stopped for?'

Keith didn't reply. Instead he wrapped his arms around the ladder and squeezed his eyes tightly shut.

'Keith,' Gwen said urgently, glancing past him at the slowly ascending zombie, whose grey, slug-like eyes were rolled most of the way up into its head. 'Come on, Keith. Just another few steps and you'll be safe.'

But Keith shook his head, like a small child refusing a mouthful of food.

Gwen felt panic rushing through her. If Keith didn't move in the next few seconds, Rhys was dead. She wondered what she could say to encourage him – and then all at once she felt herself being elbowed aside by Naomi, who thrust her face out of the attic entrance and glared down at her husband.

'*For God's sake, Keith!*' she yelled. '*What the sodding hell are you playing at? Get up here NOW!*'

Keith's eyes opened as if he had been startled from a dream, and he blinked up into his wife's furious face. Next moment he unwrapped his arms from the ladder and hauled himself upwards. Behind him, Rhys started to climb again too, urging Keith to go faster. He glanced behind him, and his heart lurched.

The lead zombie was now at the top of the stairs, no more than half a dozen paces away. Rhys scrambled up another couple of rungs, digging his shoulder into Keith's buttocks and pushing hard.

'Hurry up, mate,' he said, 'or I'll be dinner in a minute.'

Hands reached down to grab Keith and haul him into the attic. With the way suddenly clear, Rhys scrambled up the ladder, trying to stay calm and focus on not missing his footing.

It was hard to ignore the impulse to look back, however.

The dragging footsteps behind him were now horribly close, and the spoiled-meat stink of the creatures was filling his nostrils. He could hear them too, the sigh and wheeze of dead air passing through their rotting bodies, like the moaning of wind through a desolate mountain range. He glanced up, saw Gwen's anguished face framed by her raven-black hair, her hand stretching down towards him.

'Come on, Rhys,' she said. 'Come on, love. Nearly there.'

Rhys reached up to take his wife's hand – and at that moment another hand reached up from below and curled around his ankle. It was damp, that hand, and cold, but it was strong too. Rhys yelled and kicked out, but the hand only tightened its grip. He felt himself yanked backwards, and had to cling to the ladder to stop himself from falling. Above him he saw Gwen's face twist in horror and fury, saw her reach into her jacket and pull out her gun.

She shouted something, but he wasn't sure what it was. He thought she was maybe telling him to duck, to move out of the way. He flattened himself against the ladder, clinging to it the way Keith had clung to it seconds earlier. Next moment there was a roaring explosion by his ear, so loud that it not only deafened him, but sent a flash of light through his head like a bolt of lightning. He felt a split second's heat, and smelled something like scorched metal. Then abruptly the grip around his ankle loosened, though oddly Rhys could still feel the touch of the dead thing's unpleasantly yielding fingers.

He looked down, and saw that the hand was indeed still curled around his ankle – but that it was no longer attached to a body. The zombie, its foreshortened right arm a splintered mass of bone and meat, was sprawled at the bottom of the ladder, struggling to sit up. Repulsed, Rhys shook his leg, and the hand slid away from his ankle like a dead crab and fell to the ground below. More zombies were shuffling along the landing now, reaching out for him. He scrambled up the ladder and through the gap in the ceiling.

As soon as he was through, Gwen pointed her gun down through the hole and pulled the trigger. The head of a zombie which had reached the ladder disintegrated and it fell backwards. With Rhys's help, Gwen hauled the ladder up into the attic and slammed the panel into place.

They sat there in the dark, wheezing and gasping.

Finally Gwen said, 'We're safe.'

In the gloom, Naomi scowled at her.

'We're trapped, you mean,' she said.

Andy and Sophie sat side by side on the settee, munching slice after slice of cheese on toast. They had been amazed to discover how hungry they both were – and this despite the fact that Sophie had declared that the piccalilli with which Andy had coated his cheese 'smelled like puke'.

'You think this is bad,' Andy said around a mouthful of food, 'I had a mate who used to bring cheese and marmalade sandwiches to work every day.'

Sophie licked butter off her fingers and took a swig of tea. 'I tried tuna and banana once,' she said.

Andy grimaced. 'That's *disgusting*. What did it taste like?'

'It wasn't so bad once I put the ketchup on.'

'You never—' he began, and then he saw the expression on her face. 'You're pulling my leg, aren't you?'

'A bit,' she admitted. 'It was soy sauce, not ketchup.'

Andy laughed – though, as with every other rare and spontaneous outburst of humour this evening, the sound died quickly. It felt almost disrespectful to laugh after everything they had seen and experienced tonight and, whenever either of them did, it was invariably followed by a guilty and embarrassed silence.

Sure enough, for a minute or two they sat without speaking, crunching toast and listening to the thumping and writhing of Dawn on the floor of the bedroom, struggling tirelessly against her bonds.

Eventually Andy said, 'Um… Sophie?'

'Yeah?'

'I don't suppose… once all this is over, I mean… you wouldn't fancy going out for a drink or something, would you?'

Sophie looked at him, startled – and abruptly she began to giggle. Then, just as abruptly, the giggles became sobs and suddenly she was weeping, the tears running down her face.

Andy picked up a napkin from the low table in front of the settee and handed it to her with a guilty smile.

'Must admit I've never had *that* reaction before,' he said.

'Oh… sorry,' Ianto said, walking into the Boardroom and instantly turning on his heel to walk out again.

Sarah laughed. 'Don't be daft, I'm only breastfeeding. I'll stop if it makes you uncomfortable.'

Ianto turned back to face her with a stiff smile. Scrupulously maintaining eye contact, he said, 'Oh no, no. Not at all. You feed away. It's… um… not a problem.'

She smiled. 'It's OK. Really. He's about finished anyway.' Gently she removed the baby from her breast. He grizzled for a moment, then began sucking his fingers.

'So… how are you?' Ianto asked.

'I'm fine. Sore and tired, obviously, but apart from that…' She frowned slightly. 'How's Trys?'

'He's sleeping,' said Ianto quickly, thinking of her husband in the cells downstairs, staring stupidly out through the transparent wall, and occasionally blundering into it, unable to work out why he couldn't get to his prey.

'Still?' Sarah said.

'Well, we gave him some pretty strong sedatives.'

She sighed. 'I'm dying for him to see our son.'

'And he will,' Ianto said, hoping desperately that he was right. 'It won't be long now.'

He looked around, rubbing his hands together self-consciously. 'I, er, just came to see if you needed anything. Jack and I have to pop out for a bit.'

'Pop out?' she repeated, alarmed. 'You're not leaving me alone again?'

'No,' said Ianto. 'Well… not for long. We'll be back before you know it.'

'But where are you going?'

'We think we've got a lead on what's causing this… outbreak. We're just going to check it out.'

'But what if something happens while you're away?'

'It won't,' he said firmly. He produced a mobile from his pocket and handed it to her. 'My number's on there. Call me if you have any problems. Not that you will.'

She took the phone, but still looked worried. 'I'm really not happy about this.'

'You'll be perfectly safe,' Ianto assured her. 'Nothing can get in here. It's the most secure place in Cardiff.'

Gwen put her phone back in her pocket.

'What did Jack say?' Rhys asked.

'He said he and Ianto have got a lead on what's happening. They're on their way to St Helen's Hospital.'

'Why? What's at St Helen's Hospital?'

Gwen glanced at the Samuelses. It was clear she didn't want to discuss the situation in front of them – or, more particularly, in front of Naomi Samuels, who was not the most open-minded of people.

'Long story,' she said. 'I said we'd meet them there if we could.'

Rhys raised his eyebrows. 'How we gonna do that, love? We're stuck here for the time being.'

'Who are these people you're talking about?' Keith asked.

'Colleagues of mine,' said Gwen.

'Fellow spooks, you mean?'

'We're not spooks. But… yeah, that kind of thing.'

She lapsed into silence, thinking. From below came the sound of dozens of zombies, blundering and shuffling about.

'Not very bright, are they?' Rhys said. 'They can't even work out how to get up here.'

'That's why we're going to win,' said Gwen, reloading her gun.

'Win?' Naomi said sourly. 'And how are we going to do that then?'

In the dusty gloom of the attic, Naomi's face was a pallid mask of pinched, nervy anger. Gwen bit back on her impulse to snap the woman's head off, telling herself yet again that Naomi was just scared – and with good reason.

'We'll find a way,' she said.

'What the hell is that supposed to *mean*?' Naomi demanded. 'It doesn't *mean* anything.'

'Calm down, love,' Keith said placatingly. 'This isn't Gwen's fault.'

'She brought those things here, didn't she? Her and her boyfriend.'

'I'm her husband, actually,' said Rhys. He had wandered over to the grimy skylight in the roof, and was fiddling with his mobile.

'And we didn't *bring* them here,' Gwen said, trying not to get angry. 'Cardiff's overrun with them. It's chaos out there.'

'But they wouldn't have bothered us if you hadn't turned up,' Naomi retorted.

'We don't know that, love,' said Keith.

Gwen flashed Jasmine a reassuring smile. The little girl was clutching her yellow rabbit and eyeing the bickering adults with trepidation.

'Keith's right,' said Rhys. 'If those things had got in while you were asleep you'd have been torn apart in your beds.'

He noticed Gwen glance meaningfully at Jasmine and give a quick shake of the head. He shrugged.

'Sorry, Gwen, but it's true. You're a lot safer up here. Come *on*.'

This last remark was directed at his phone, which he was now holding above his head, as though making an offering to the moon.

'What are you doing, Rhys?' said Gwen irritably.

'I'm trying to get a decent signal on this bloody thing.'

'Why?'

'Why do you think? I want to make a call.'

Frustrated, he lifted the security bar on the window and shoved it open, then thrust the hand that was holding the mobile out into the drizzly night.

'Bingo!' he exclaimed.

'Who are you wanting to call anyway?' said Gwen. 'Rentokil?'

He gave her the look a teacher might give a facetious pupil. 'I'm calling in a favour,' he said. 'It's a bit of a long shot, but you never know.'

The pod, which was sitting in an open containment case on Ianto's lap, was going crazy, pulsing brighter and more fiercely as they neared the hospital. The coloured lights flickering just beneath the surface of its opaque skin were moving so rapidly that Ianto couldn't keep track of them. The pod's rate of regeneration was increasing too; indeed, Ianto fancied he could now see the silvery orb repairing itself before his eyes. He was watching it, mesmerised, when the SUV slammed into something, jolting him out of his reverie.

'Zombie roadkill,' said Jack. 'Couldn't be helped. He stepped right out in front of me.'

Ianto glanced into the rear-view mirror, to see a dark smear on the road behind them.

'There's no need to sound so happy about it,' he said. 'I worry about you sometimes.'

Jack grinned. 'What can I say? I enjoy my work.'

They were very close to the hospital now. The drive through Cardiff had been a journey through a nightmare landscape. Even in the couple of hours they had been in the Hub, the number of zombies had increased dramatically. They were *everywhere*, filling the streets, aimlessly shuffling. Cardiff had become a city of the dead.

Jack had managed to avoid most of them, though some

had had to be nudged aside. Ianto knew that if Jack had had his way, he would have simply ploughed through the lot of them.

'It's not like they're *real*,' he had told Ianto, when Ianto had asked him to slow down and be careful, 'and this baby is big enough and tough enough to cope.'

'That's not the point,' Ianto said. 'You're not the one who has to clean up the mess afterwards.'

It didn't help that the creatures seemed so interested in the pod. Whether it was the flashing lights or something more intrinsic, it certainly seemed to spark a reaction. *Or maybe it's just us*, thought Ianto. *Maybe it's just the fact that we're the only thing apart from themselves that's moving.* Certainly, wherever they went, the dead would converge on them, arms outstretched and something like… what? eagerness? recognition? in their otherwise glazed eyes.

At last they turned a corner, and there was the hospital entrance, a hundred metres ahead of them.

'Weird,' said Jack.

'What is?'

'Look around. What d'you see?'

Ianto peered through the windscreen. It was a leafy street in a nice part of town. Big houses on the left; the hospital grounds, flanked by high hedges, on the right.

At first he didn't see what Jack was getting at, and then he realised. 'Oh,' he said. 'No zombies.'

'A coupla streets behind us it was wall to wall, but here there's nothing,' said Jack. 'Pretty odd, wouldn't you say?'

Ianto remained silent. It was only when Jack swung the SUV through the gates leading in to the multi-level car park and they saw the brightly lit building before them that the mystery of the missing zombies was solved.

The creatures were standing in rows, several layers deep, forming a cordon around the building. There were literally hundreds of them, and they were motionless and eerily silent.

'My God,' breathed Ianto. On his lap, the pod was pulsing more fiercely than ever.

Jack looked across at Ianto and raised an eyebrow. 'No prizes for guessing what they're guarding,' he said.

It was odd in a way, but the constant state of tension, of apprehension, had become boring after a while. Tired of the crush of people in Reception, and more particularly of their endless theorising and analysing, Rianne and Nina had retreated to the empty maternity ward, and were now sitting in the semi-darkness, staring out over the car park, cradling mugs of tea.

They hadn't talked much in the last half-hour or so. In fact, Nina had spent much of the time dozing. A nurse had cleaned and re-bandaged her leg for her; despite what Nina's friends had thought, she hadn't needed stitches.

'I wonder what happened to the Thomases,' Rianne said.

'Huh?' Once again, Nina's eyes had been drooping closed. Rianne reached out and gently took the half-empty mug out of her hands.

'Sarah Thomas. She's one of my ladies. She phoned earlier this evening to say she'd gone into labour. I hope she's all right.'

Before Nina could rouse herself to answer, the faint screech of brakes from outside drew Rianne to the window. At the top end of the car park was a big shiny-black vehicle, all lit up like a Christmas tree. In fact, it was *pulsing* with light, as if it contained some kind of mobile disco.

Rianne tensed. Clearly the occupants of the vehicle had seen the creatures massed around the hospital. *Turn back*, she urged them silently, *turn back.*

The big black vehicle began to rumble forward.

'No!' Rianne said, loud enough to snap Nina fully awake.

'Wassamatter?' Nina muttered.

Rianne gestured at the approaching vehicle in dismay. 'Another lamb to the slaughter.'

Nina hauled herself out of her chair and hobbled across to stand beside Rianne. They watched the big black car edging towards the hospital, rippling and strobing with inner light, almost as if it *wanted* to draw attention to itself.

The creatures encircling the hospital had been still and silent for some time, but now twenty or more of them jerked into motion and peeled away from the main throng, shuffling towards the newcomers.

'Get away from here. Get away,' Rianne urged, her fists clenched in dreadful anticipation.

Nina's voice was as bleak as her words. 'Whoever they are, they don't stand a chance.'

In his hospital bed, Oscar Phillips thrashed and writhed. His lips curled back over clenched teeth gleaming with spittle, and his eyes rolled madly behind their closed lids.

FOURTEEN

'This isn't good,' Ianto said nervously as zombies swarmed over the SUV.

Jack, however, seemed unperturbed. 'Relax, Ianto,' he said. 'This thing's tougher than a tank. There's no way in hell they can get in.'

'Yes, but there's no way we can get out either,' Ianto replied. 'In fact, there's so many of them I doubt we could even drive through.'

Jack acknowledged the observation with a shrug. 'There *is* that, I guess.'

He nodded at the orb, pulsing madly in the box on Ianto's lap.

'Maybe buddy boy there will protect us.'

'Or maybe they'll tear us apart to get to it,' Ianto said. 'It certainly seems to have agitated them.'

It was true. In the presence of the pod, the zombies seemed more animated, more ferocious than usual. They were crawling all over the SUV, pounding and scrabbling at the windows, leaving greasy smears of themselves behind. Their rotting faces glared in at Jack and Ianto, the pod's light flashing silver in their lifeless eyes.

Jack unholstered his Webley. 'Only one way to find out,' he said.

Ianto blanched. 'You're not going out there?'

As ever, Jack seemed to relish the prospect of extreme danger. 'It's either that or sit here till doomsday.'

'But you'll be killed,' Ianto said.

Jack shrugged. 'So what's new?'

'This is different, Jack, and you know it. They'll tear you apart. They'll *eat* you.'

Jack was unmoved. 'Well, you know what they say about life – the best way to enjoy it is to fill it with new experiences.' He held out his hand. 'Give me the pod, Ianto.'

'This is madness, Jack,' Ianto protested.

Jack's face was set, determined. 'Give me the pod,' he repeated.

Ianto sighed, momentarily undecided, and then unhappily he handed the box over to Jack. Jack lifted out the pulsing pod and slipped it into an inside pocket of his greatcoat. He tossed the box onto the back seat, then leaned forward, pulled Ianto towards him and kissed him on the forehead.

'You wait for me here. If I don't manage to find Oscar

and stop all this… well, just do what you can. Drive. Get back to the Hub.'

But Ianto shook his head, suddenly decisive. 'No. If you're going, I'm coming with you.'

'No way,' Jack said. 'My own stupidity I can live with. I'm not having you risking *your* life.'

Now it was Ianto's turn to look determined. Drawing his gun, he said, 'It's my decision, Jack. I chose to do this job. I know what the risks are.'

Jack looked as though he *wanted* to argue, but couldn't find a firm basis from which to do so. In the end he simply flapped a hand at Ianto and said, 'OK. If that's what you want, let's *both* go out in a blaze of glory. You ready?'

'Ready,' Ianto said grimly.

'Now!' Jack shouted.

They shoved their doors open simultaneously, causing zombies to tumble back like skittles. Instantly more of the creatures surged forward to fill the gap, teeth bared and eyes staring, hands reaching out.

Ianto pointed his gun and started shooting. And horrible as it was to see fleshless skulls shattering into fragments and heads disintegrating into bloody meat before his eyes, he *continued* shooting, trying to console himself with the knowledge that the creatures weren't real, that they felt no pain, that this was, in effect, nothing but a three-dimensional – albeit potentially lethal – computer game.

He was still shooting as he swung his legs from the SUV and stood up. And behind him he was aware that

Jack was shooting too, the sharper crack of his Webley revolver underpinning the deafening boom of Ianto's semi-automatic.

Zombies fell in swathes before him, but they kept coming out of the darkness, kept pushing him back. One grabbed at him from the roof of the SUV; he turned and shot it from point-blank range.

Another swiped at his face, raking jagged fingernails down his cheek, before he was able to swivel and shoot it in the throat.

Yet another, a goth girl with black lipstick, panda eyes, and entrails leaking from a festering wound in her stomach, latched on to his left arm and sunk her teeth into his shoulder. He dislodged her by slamming her into the side of the SUV before she could break the skin, and then shooting her through her spiky forest of black hair while she was scrabbling on the ground.

At last the inevitable happened. While Ianto was pointing his gun, a flailing arm knocked the weapon from his hand. Ianto watched in despair as it flew through the air and clattered to the ground, among the shuffling feet of the walking dead.

Oh God, this is it, he thought as they surged towards him. He turned, grabbed the still-open door of the SUV and used it to haul himself up towards the roof of the vehicle, in the final desperate hope that he might be able to defend himself better from up there.

Just as he reached the roof, kicking out at hands that were snatching at his legs, he became aware of three things simultaneously: an incredibly bright light, a loud, clattering whirr, and a raging wind that swooped down on him from nowhere. The light dazzled him, and the wind knocked the breath from his body and threatened to wrench him from his precarious perch. Clinging on for dear life, Ianto dropped to all fours and managed, with extreme difficulty, to turn his head.

For a second or two the light was so blinding that he couldn't work out what he was looking at. Hovering in the air above the SUV was what appeared to be an illuminated metal wall painted in white and orange stripes. Then Ianto saw landing wheels and the whickering blur of rotor blades, and suddenly realised he was staring at the underside of a helicopter. It had a bright red nose and tail, and a white body. The words 'COASTGUARD RESCUE' were printed in bold black capitals on the fuselage side of the aircraft.

Ianto sensed scrabbling movement beside him and twisted his head again, thinking that one of the zombies had climbed up after him. But it was Jack, bathed in the glare from above, and with rainbow light from the pod pulsing through his thick coat, still firing his Webley into the throng below. He turned briefly and grinned, hair flapping wildly around his head. He shouted something about 'cavalry', but the roar of the helicopter was too loud for Ianto to make out his words properly.

Then Ianto saw a line descending from the side door of the helicopter, and attached to the line was Gwen, black hair flying and leather jacket gleaming, haloed by the helicopter spotlight. Gwen was pointing her gun and taking potshots at the zombies below. Despite the fierce wind, Jack stood up on the roof of the SUV, waving and laughing.

Gwen was grinning too when she alighted on the roof of the SUV.

'Hello, boys,' she shouted. 'Having fun?'

'We are now,' Jack laughed, and hugged her tightly. Then in the same movement he swivelled and shot a zombie, which had poked its head over the edge of the roof. It fell back without a sound.

'Right,' Gwen yelled. 'Who's first?'

'Ianto,' Jack said decisively.

When Ianto looked about to protest, Jack shouted, 'You're mortal and you don't have a weapon.'

Ianto couldn't argue with that. 'Fair enough,' he said.

He was attached to the supplementary line and winched aboard the helicopter, rising up through the buffeting wind and the roar of the massive engines. It was roomy inside, and contained more people than he'd been expecting – Rhys, for one, and a rather dazed-looking family of three.

A few minutes later, Jack too was aboard. The three of them had a brief but joyful reunion.

'How the hell did you wangle this?' Jack marvelled, grinning from ear to ear. 'You're amazing, you know that?'

Gwen indicated Rhys, who was standing a little apart from the trio, watching them with an indulgent expression. 'Actually it wasn't me,' she said, 'it was Rhys.'

'*Rhys?*' Jack tried his best not to look astonished.

Rhys nodded at the helmeted pilot. 'That's Nobby. He's a mate of mine. He owed me a favour.'

'Musta been a really big one,' said Jack.

'Let's just say it involved a cocktail waitress and a bottle of vodka.'

Jack laughed uproariously and threw his arms around Rhys in a bear hug. Rhys looked startled, but pleased.

Ianto noticed the family all staring with astonishment at Jack, whose entire body seemed to be pulsing with light beneath his greatcoat.

Straight-faced, he said, 'Just ignore him. He likes to show off. He's not even a real American.'

FIFTEEN

Less than a minute later, the helicopter alighted on the flat roof of the hospital. Jack was standing by the still-open door, leaning out as though taking the air, his greatcoat flapping like a cape.

As the aircraft touched down, he turned back and said, 'Gwen, Ianto, with me. The rest of you, wait here.'

Rhys jumped up from his seat. 'No chance,' he said. 'I'm coming with you.'

Jack shook his head. 'Not this time, Rhys.'

'You can't stop me,' Rhys said, glancing at Gwen, as if for support. 'I've come this far. I want to see it through to the end.'

'You don't have a weapon,' said Jack.

'Neither does Ianto,' said Gwen, earning herself a frown of annoyance from Jack. Undeterred, she said, 'If it hadn't been for Rhys, you and Ianto would've been torn apart down there, and we'd still be stuck in the Samuels's attic. He's saved the lot of us.'

A little acidly, Jack said, 'I thought you, of all people, would want him kept safe.'

'Of course I do!' snapped Gwen. 'But he wants me kept safe too. I just think, after all we've been through, that it's not fair to exclude him now.'

Jack rolled his eyes. 'OK. But he's your responsibility.'

Gwen smiled at Rhys. 'As always,' she said.

Rianne clapped her hands as the helicopter rose into the air with its passengers safely aboard. 'They got away!' she exclaimed gleefully. 'Oh, thank God!'

Nina, standing beside her, said thoughtfully, 'They had guns. I wonder who they were.'

'Police?' suggested Rianne.

'They didn't look like police. They looked like… I don't know. Special agents or something.'

'Maybe the government have brought them in to sort things out,' Rianne suggested.

'Maybe,' said Nina. 'But what was that glowing thing? Some sort of weapon, do you think?'

'I don't know,' said Rianne, then pointed out of the window. 'Look, those things are on the move.'

Acting as one, the zombies had turned from the SUV and were now heading back towards the hospital as fast as their individual infirmities would allow. Seconds later the two women looked at each other in horror as, from several floors below, they heard the faint but unmistakable sound of shattering glass.

'So where's Oscar?' Gwen asked.

They were in the hospital, heading downwards. Jack had his PDA in his hand and was using it to pinpoint energy readings inside the building which might echo those from the pod.

'Configuring now... Got him!' he cried. 'He's three floors below us.'

'And you're sure that's him?' said Rhys.

'No one else it could be,' Jack replied, and raced down the stairs.

At ground level, it was absolute chaos. People screamed and ran in all directions as zombies smashed their way into the building. After a long stalemate, it was as though the creatures had suddenly received the signal to attack. Without warning they had surged forward, hurling themselves against the glass entrance doors. The crush of bodies had caused the thick glass first to crack, and then to shatter inwards. The first few rows of zombies had all but sacrificed themselves to gain access to the building, falling forward as the doors gave way. Many had been slashed open by jagged glass, and then trampled underfoot by the creatures behind them. Some of the fallen, their bodies pin-cushioned by glass shards, still struggled to drag themselves along, hampered by terrible wounds or shattered limbs.

Stuck in his wheelchair, Alexander Martin gripped the armrests with claw-like hands and stared in disbelief as what looked like the occupants of every morgue and graveyard in Cardiff lurched and staggered and crawled towards him. His attendant nurse, an effete and tiresome little shit called Ben, had run off screaming with the rest of the cowards, leaving Alexander to fend for himself.

Making a mental note to hunt down and decapitate Ben if, by some miracle, he managed to survive this impossible and absurd night, the old man's rheumy eyes darted right and left, searching for possible escape routes. All exits, however, were simply out of range; by the time he'd managed to get this bloody beast of a chair pointing in the right direction, the stinking hordes would be all over him.

In desperation, therefore, he looked around for something to defend himself with, but all he saw were discarded cups and water bottles, magazines and sweet wrappers. There was nothing sharp, nor even long, he could use – no walking sticks, no umbrellas. Not even a bloody biro, for Christ's sake!

Facing the inevitable was not in Alexander's nature. All his life he had been a battler, a fighter, stubborn and determined, living on his wits. His end, he had always envisaged, would be comfortable and painless. He had planned to expire gracefully between silken sheets, a beautiful woman by his side. He had never in a million years thought that he would be reduced to such ignominy. To be torn apart by something that resembled a butcher's leftovers! It was downright embarrassing.

The thing making a beeline for him at that moment was a long-haired lunk with a face like a salted slug and a big piece of glass sticking out of the middle of his forehead. Alexander pointed at a fat woman, who was cowering in her wheelchair about ten metres away, making little whimpering noises.

'Why don't you go for her, you revolting moron?' he railed. 'There's ten times more meat on her bloated carcass than you'll find on my scrawny bones.'

His words had no effect, and as Slug-Face came within touching distance, Alexander clenched his teeth in a snarl and raised his fists, ready to go down fighting…

… only for the creature to brush straight past him as though he didn't exist.

Alexander was astonished. Had the thing not seen him because he was sitting down? But when he looked around, he realised that none of the other half a dozen or so people left behind in the Reception area were being attacked either. The creatures were simply ignoring them, shuffling past without so much as a glance.

As the gruesome parade passed by, Alexander sat up a little straighter in his chair. When it became obvious that he was not going to die here, after all, he began to cackle at the sheer grotesqueness of the spectacle.

Clearly, he thought, the dead things had a definite agenda. They were all heading for somewhere specific.

But where?

***

The sign above the forbidding double doors read 'INTENSIVE CARE UNIT – AUTHORISED PERSONNEL ONLY'.

'That's us,' Jack said, and pushed the left-hand door open.

Beyond the doors was a wide corridor with an orange floor and subdued lighting. There was an empty desk halfway along, atop which was a scatter of paperwork, an open laptop, a desk lamp with a green bulb and a half-empty mug of tea. Flanking the corridor on both sides were rows of glass-fronted IC cubicles, each one large enough to contain a hospital bed and however many items of monitoring equipment each individual patient required.

'Isn't that supposed to be manned at all times?' Gwen said, nodding at the desk.

'It is,' replied Jack. 'Someone's abandoned their station.'

Ianto shook his head and tut-tutted. 'Dereliction of duty. Anyone could just walk in here.'

'Which one of these rooms is Oscar in?' asked Gwen.

Jack reached into his greatcoat. 'Let's find out, shall we?'

They all oohed as he withdrew the pod from his pocket. It was almost complete now, rippling and pulsing with the most incredible light show. Holding it in front of him, Jack walked slowly along the corridor, the others trailing in his wake. Just before he reached the nurse's desk, the pod began to emit a warbling cry, as it had done in the

Hub when the zombie had got close to it. However, the sound wasn't quite so much like an alarm this time.

'Is it singing?' Rhys asked.

'Sounds like a lament. Like it's calling out for someone,' said Ianto.

'It's beautiful,' breathed Gwen. 'Heartbreaking too.'

Jack turned to the cubicle on his right. 'Here,' he said.

Through the observation window, linked up to an IV drip and various items of monitoring equipment, they could see a slight, pale figure lying in bed. The figure was jerking and twitching, as though being subjected to a series of electric shocks. Jack pushed open the door and entered, the light from the pod making the sleeping figure's skin look cold and hard as marble. As Jack approached the bed, the figure's eyes snapped open. Then Oscar Phillips sat up straight and swivelled his head towards them.

'Hi there,' Jack said gently. 'You're Oscar, right?'

The young man didn't respond. With his wide, staring eyes and sickly complexion, he looked not unlike a zombie himself.

'Is he awake?' whispered Gwen, standing at Jack's shoulder.

Whether in response to her voice or simply reacting to the light, Oscar swung his legs stiffly out of bed and stood up.

As he did so, sensor pads tore themselves from his skin, leaving circular red marks, and the IV drip on its metal stand tottered and fell with a shattering crash. The plastic

IV bag burst open like an overripe fruit, spattering liquid across the floor. Rhys winced as the IV tube was ripped out of Oscar's arm with a spurt of blood.

Oscar seemed oblivious to all of this. He padded barefoot towards Jack and held out his hands.

'You want the pod? Is that it?' murmured Jack.

'You're not going to give it to him, are you?' asked Rhys.

'Sure. Why not?'

Jack stepped forward and placed the glowing pod carefully into Oscar's outstretched hands. Oscar came to a halt, a mildly bemused expression on his face. He looked like a blind man trying to identify something from its shape and texture. And then all at once his throat bulged, like that of a bullfrog, and his mouth opened wider than seemed possible.

'Oh my God,' muttered Gwen.

'What the hell's *that*?' exclaimed Rhys.

Something emerged from Oscar's mouth, something grey and jelly-like. It resembled an overlong tongue, or perhaps a gigantic glistening slug. It oozed from between Oscar's lips, moved sinuously through the air, like a snake swimming through water, and entered the pod.

There was a sudden surge of light and the pod sealed itself before their eyes, becoming whole again. It rose into the air, hovering, like a mini-sun.

'What now?' wondered Ianto nervously.

'It looks as though it's getting its bearings,' whispered Gwen.

Jack stepped forward.

'My name is Captain Jack Harkness. I represent the people of Earth. And I really think we need to talk.'

'People of Earth, is it?' whispered Rhys to Gwen. 'Pompous git.'

She elbowed him in the ribs.

As if responding to Jack's proclamation, the pod drifted down and latched itself to Oscar's forehead. Oscar went momentarily rigid, his eyes and mouth widening in shock.

Then his features relaxed and he rotated his jaw a few times, as though to check it was in working order. When he spoke, the voice that emerged was fluting and ethereal, almost playful.

'Greetings, Captain Jack Harkness,' he said. 'I am Leet. I am a child of the Dellacoi. I will use the language of the Oscarphillips to communicate with you.'

'Nice to meet you, Leet,' Jack said neutrally. 'You mind telling me what you're doing here?'

Oscar stared straight ahead, his mouth moving with an odd stiffness as the alien spoke through him. 'I was riding the time winds when I was snatched away and hurled into this world. My life-shell was damaged on impact. In order to survive I sought refuge in this life form.'

'So you're a parasite?' Jack said.

'I am a symbiont,' replied the alien with no trace of indignation. 'The relationship between myself and the Oscarphillips has been a mutually beneficial one. Without me the Oscarphillips would not have survived, and without the Oscarphillips I would have perished in the cold wastes of this planet.'

'So you've been keeping each other alive for the past three months?' said Ianto.

'Three months, yes. I have learned this time frame from the Oscarphillips. For three months our consciousnesses have been linked, our thoughts, dreams and desires merging into one.'

'So what's with the night of zombie mayhem?' Jack asked. 'I'm guessing you're responsible for that?'

'Two nights ago,' the Dellacoi replied, 'I heard the call of my life-shell. I used images from the most recent memories of the Oscarphillips to create search units so that my life-shell and I could be reunited. However, the memories of the Oscarphillips proved too… volatile. Once I had activated the units, I found I could not control them. And so, in order to contain the units and limit the damage, I created a barrier around this place, this… Cardiff.'

'And you created them how?' asked Ianto.

For the first time the Dellacoi sounded puzzled. 'By thinking them. Isn't this how you create your world? Your buildings and your TV sets, your cars and your computers?'

Gwen glanced at Jack, and knew that he was thinking the same as she was: a species that could create a world of solid objects out of pure thought! If the Dellacoi proved hostile there would be no stopping it.

Ignoring the alien's question, Jack said, 'So tell me,

Leet, how do we get rid of these units of yours? How do we get things back to normal?'

The Dellacoi said, 'The units are no longer mine. They belong to the Oscarphillips. Only the Oscarphillips can contain them.'

Before Jack could respond, there was a bang as the double doors leading into the Intensive Care Unit were flung open. Gwen and Jack drew their guns.

'Time out!' Jack shouted. 'Arm yourselves, people!'

Rhys had left his golf club behind in the mad scramble up to the Samuels's attic, so he picked up the metal IV stand. Ianto looked around frantically, then ran across to a metal-framed chair next to the room's tall window and snatched it up, holding it in front of him like a lion tamer.

There was a blundering rush of movement in the corridor, and suddenly zombies were crowding against the observation windows of the IC unit, their ravaged faces savage now, eyes glaring, driven by the primitive urge to protect their creator.

Snarling and groaning, the creatures threw themselves against the door and windows, all of which cracked and then burst inwards in a shower of glass.

The walking dead flooded into the room, and as Jack and Gwen began firing, and Rhys and Ianto fended off attackers with their makeshift weapons, the Dellacoi pod rose from Oscar's forehead, flared and vanished. Instantly Oscar's eyes slid closed and he collapsed to the floor with a sleepy groan.

Gwen roared through her bared teeth as she pumped bullet after bullet into the advancing army of living dead. However, it quickly became obvious that she was fighting a losing battle. Despite the ever-growing pile of rotting corpses, the creatures just kept on coming, a seemingly endless stream of them, intent on tearing her apart.

She fired again, and another zombie fell, the bullet ripping half of its head away, then spun to her left to take out a bloated teenager in a supermarket tabard. As she did, a boy no older than four, his mouth and hands a mess of gore, threw himself at her leg like a pit bull terrier. Caught by surprise, Gwen stumbled and fell heavily, cracking her shoulder on the metal frame of the bed with enough force to jar the gun out of her hand. She had no time to see where it went because the boy was on her in an instant, his bloody hands climbing her body, his teeth gnashing as he homed in on her throat.

She held him off as best she could, but he was like an eel – slippery, vicious and immensely strong. She was vaguely aware of other zombies crowding around her, reaching down with their clawed and rotting hands.

In rage and terror, Gwen screamed…

SIXTEEN

Deep down, in the dark and the quiet, Oscar and his friend Leet were talking. Leet had confessed how he had borrowed and moulded Oscar's memories without his permission, and how those memories had subsequently escaped, replicating and mutating like a virus, turning bad.

'Oscar,' Leet said to him – and to Oscar he seemed to speak in thought bubbles, like in a comic book – 'only you can save the world. It's up to you to put it right.'

Oscar nodded slowly, his face grim and determined. 'Leave it to me, Leet,' he said authoritatively. And then he rather spoiled it by asking, 'What do I do?'

So Leet told him, and now Oscar was rushing up towards the light, rushing and rushing, faster and faster. The light was getting bigger. First, it was the size of a pinprick; then an eye; then a football; and then suddenly it was the size of an entire planet.

Oscar burst back into the world with a sound like a thunderclap. He opened his eyes and there on the floor, just a few inches from his outstretched hand, was the gun, exactly where Leet had told him it would be. He curled his hand around it, and it felt good, it felt *right*. And then, with one bound, he was on his feet and looking around him, taking in everything in an instant with his super-sight.

Everything Leet had told him was true. His memories were out of his head, and out of control. He raised his hands and shouted, '*Stop!*'

And the memories *did* stop. They stopped and they looked at him, as if waiting to be told what to do next. And the four people – the four *real* people – looked at him as well: the smart man with the chair; the chubby man with the metal stand; the handsome man in the long coat; the black-haired girl on the floor, who immediately scrambled to her feet and shouldered her way out of the memories which were crowding around her.

'Sorry,' Oscar said to them, and then he turned and pointed the gun at the tall window opposite the door. He pulled the trigger, and the window, blind and curtains and all, exploded outwards into the night.

A voice roared, '*Stop!*' and, incredibly, the zombies obeyed. The ferocious child pushed itself away from Gwen and stood beside her, almost to attention. The zombies which had been reaching down to tear her apart straightened up. Eerily, they all turned their heads towards the source of the sound. Exhausted, bedraggled and covered in bloody handprints, Gwen turned *her* head too.

She saw Oscar Phillips standing in the middle of the room, amid the chaos, with a gun – *her* gun – in his hand. His eyes were shining and his face was serene. When his gaze passed briefly over her she shivered, and then she scrambled to her feet.

'Sorry,' Oscar said, and then he turned and pointed the gun at the window. He pulled the trigger and the glass shattered, the impact causing the blind and the curtains to go flailing out into the darkness in the wake of the falling glass.

Gwen's attention was still focused on the jagged remains of the window when Oscar started to run towards it. He ran fast, with no trace of post-coma lethargy or muscle wastage, zombies stepping aside to allow him passage. Realising what he was doing, Gwen yelled, '*No!*' and leaped forward to stop him. But Jack leaped at the same moment, grabbing her arm and hauling her back. She could only watch in horror as Oscar dived head first out of the window, his thin, pyjama-clad body sailing into the night.

For a moment, like the Darling children from Peter Pan, he looked as though he might fly. And then his body twisted and he plummeted towards the earth.

Angrily, Gwen tore herself free of Jack, ran to the window and looked down. Oscar's twisted, broken body lay in a spreading pool of blood on the concrete far below. She heard gasps of shock and surprise behind her, and turned round.

Only Jack, Ianto and Rhys stood there on the blood-smeared floor, amid the broken glass and overturned furniture. All that was left of the zombies were a few spirals of glittering light, which rose into the air and disappeared.

Rhys dropped the metal IV stand, which clattered to the floor. Ianto put down the chair he was holding and sank shakily into it.

'They just… melted away,' said Rhys. 'Into, like… twinkly little balls of light.'

'Stardust,' muttered Ianto.

Jack reached into the pocket of his greatcoat and withdrew a creased and crumpled handbill, which he held out for them all to see.

'I think the *All-Night Zombie Horror Show* is officially over,' he said.

SEVENTEEN

'Help!' came the shout from the bedroom.

Andy jerked awake, and realised that he was slumped on the settee with his arm around the shoulders of a sleeping Sophie. His hand was numb and his back was aching. He tried to sit up without disturbing her, but she stirred anyway.

'Wazzit?' she mumbled.

'Did you hear someone shouting just now?' asked Andy. 'Or did I dream it?'

As if in response, the shout came again. 'Help! Is anybody there? Can anyone hear me?'

'That's Dawn,' Andy said, detaching himself from Sophie and rising to his feet.

Sophie used an arm to push her blonde hair out of her face. 'What do you mean?'

'That's Dawn shouting. She sounds normal.' He ran out of the room and down the corridor to the bedroom.

'Dawn,' he shouted, tugging at the flex he had tied around the door handle. 'Dawn, it's Andy. Are you OK?'

'Andy,' she said, sounding half-relieved and half-angry. 'Where am I? What the hell's going on? Why am I tied up?'

Andy turned to grin at Sophie, who was padding along the corridor, yawning and wiping sleep out of her eyes.

'It's a bit of a long story,' he said.

Trys Thomas woke up shouting and thrashing. He had had the most terrible dreams. He sat up and looked around him, bewildered and terrified.

Where was he? In some kind of dungeon? Three of the four walls of the room – the *cell* – in which he was lying were made of rough, dank stone. The fourth wall appeared to be some kind of thick transparent plastic with neat air-holes drilled into it. Beyond the plastic was what looked like part of a corridor or walkway with another stone wall beyond that. The entire area was soaked in dim reddish lighting, and there were... sounds coming from somewhere nearby. Horrible, animal-like sounds. Grunting and shuffling. Trys's heart started to race and he felt panic building inside him.

That was when he noticed the mobile phone. It was propped up against the bottom-left corner of the transparent plastic wall. Stuck on the wall beside the phone was a post-it note on which someone had written:

Press 1. Licking his lips, Trys scurried across to the phone and snatched it up. He pressed 1.

Almost immediately a voice said, 'Hello? Is that Trys?'

Trys's voice was little more than a croak. 'Who's this?'

'My name's Ianto Jones,' said the voice. 'How are you feeling?'

'Where the bloody hell am I?' Trys demanded.

The man who had called himself Ianto Jones sighed. 'Listen, I know you're confused and probably a bit scared, but trust me, you're perfectly safe and we'll be coming to let you out in… oh, about twenty minutes. So just sit tight, OK? I'll explain everything when I get there.'

'Where's my wife?' asked Trys. 'Where's Sarah?'

'She's fine. She's healthy.'

'And the baby? Has she—'

'He's fine too.'

'He?' said Trys in a kind of wonder.

'Yes. You're a dad, Mr Thomas. Congratulations. See you soon.'

Nobby groaned. As if things weren't bad enough, that bloody Samuels woman was doing his head in. Her husband was nice, but she was like sodding whiplash. Moaning and complaining. Constantly demanding to know what was going on, and what would happen to them. Why couldn't she just accept that Nobby was as much in the dark as they were?

First he'd heard of all this zombie nonsense was when Rhys had called him up at piss-off o'clock and told him he needed serious payback for that little slip-up with the cocktail waitress. Well, fair enough. But if anyone found out Nobby had taken the chopper without proper authorisation he'd be in the brown stuff up to his neck, valiant rescue or not. Rhys was a good mate and all, but this was taking friendship a bit too far.

In the end what it came down to for Nobby was a choice between his job and his marriage. And what had finally swung it was Rhys's dead serious insistence that for him and Gwen (ah, gorgeous Gwen) Nobby's involvement might literally be a matter of life and death. But if Rhys had warned him one of the people he'd be rescuing was Cruella De Vil's more obnoxious sister, he might have thought again.

She was giving him earache again now, demanding to know how long they were going to be stuck up here on this roof. Nobby held up a hand to quieten her as his mobile went, playing the theme tune from *The A-Team*. He saw Rhys's name flash up.

'Yeah?' he said gruffly.

'It's over, mate,' said Rhys. 'We've sorted it.'

'Good for you,' said Nobby sarcastically.

'You can head off if you want,' Rhys told him. 'Drop your passengers off on the way. I'll find my own way home from here.'

'That's big of you,' muttered Nobby.

'Oh, and mate?' Rhys said.

'Yeah?'

'You won't get in bother for this. Trust me. I've got a

bloke here, Gwen's boss, who'll sort it. In fact, he says if anything you'll get a commendation.'

'Gwen's boss?' said Nobby. 'That flash bloke with the disco ball under his coat? Who's he, then?'

'It's… classified,' Rhys said, evidently feeling foolish for saying so.

'Your Gwen's in special ops, isn't she? All hush-hush and top secret?'

'Something like that,' said Rhys vaguely.

'You lucky bugger,' said Nobby. 'I bet it's all handcuffs and truncheons in your house.'

'Nobby,' said Rhys.

'Yeah?'

'Get yourself home, mate, and have a cold shower.'

Nobby laughed, considerably cheerier now. 'Will do, mate. See you soon.'

For a full minute after the shooting stopped, Rianne and Nina continued to cling to each other. At last Nina tentatively raised her head.

'It's gone quiet,' she said.

Carefully the two women extricated themselves from one another's embrace, as if fearful that any sudden moves might start things off all over again.

'What does that mean, do you think?' whispered Rianne.

Nina limped across to the door. 'Let's find out, shall we?'

Rianne half-held up a hand. 'Do you think that's a

good idea? What if those things are still out there?'

'We'll just have a peep,' said Nina. 'After all, we can't stay here for ever, can we?'

Rianne drew a long, shuddering breath. 'No,' she said. 'I suppose we can't.'

The two women crept to the door of the empty ward and pushed it open. Nina listened for a moment, and then stuck her head out. The corridor stretching from here to the double doors at the far end was empty and silent. It was almost as if the hospital was stunned, as if it was holding its breath, ready for the next onslaught.

'See anything?' whispered Rianne.

'No,' murmured Nina. 'Come on.'

The two of them tiptoed along the corridor to the double doors. They jumped as a baby cried in one of the connecting wards, and grinned sheepishly at each other. There was no sign of Sister Felicity Andrews and her staff. Rianne hoped that they were with the new mothers, spreading calm and reassurance, damping down the panic.

When they reached the double doors, Nina put her ear to one and listened.

'Anything?' whispered Rianne.

Nina shook her head. 'I'm going to have a look.'

Rianne clenched her fists and drew them almost unconsciously up to her breasts as Nina eased the right-hand door open.

The instant she had done so there was a thump of feet on the open stairwell beyond the lifts and a quartet of people appeared. In the lead was a handsome man in a long coat, who swept past, heading downwards without a glance.

Nina stepped out. 'Hey!' she called.

The man bringing up the rear of the group – chubby, bedraggled, friendly looking – glanced across at her.

'What's happening?' she asked.

The man smiled wryly. 'Take me about three hours to answer that one, sweetheart.'

'OK, just answer me this then – is it safe to come out?'

The man halted, hesitated briefly, then shrugged. 'Is it *ever* safe round here?' he said. Then he nodded. 'But as far as it goes… yeah. The zombies are dead. Again.'

By the time Jack, Gwen, Ianto and Rhys reached the ground floor, people were beginning to emerge from hiding. They reminded Jack of how people had looked after an air raid during the war – pale with trauma, blinking in the light, fearful of who might have been lost in the night's barrage but warily gleeful that they themselves had survived.

He and the rest of the Torchwood team moved through the huddled groups of bewildered humanity with a sense of determination, of purpose, speaking to no one. The immediate threat might have been over, but the mopping-up operation was going to take them the rest of the day.

Hearing raised voices over to his left, Jack glanced around. An elderly man in a wheelchair was ranting at a poor nurse, who looked as though she'd been through quite enough for one night. For a moment, Jack contemplated heading over, telling him to leave the poor girl alone. Then he heard the man snarl, 'Alexander Martin. *Mr* Martin to you. And don't you forget it!'

All at once Jack came to a halt, grinning in recognition. How many years had it been since he'd last seen Alexander Martin? My, but time had not been kind to the old curmudgeon.

For a moment he wondered about going over to say hi – and then decided that now was not the time. He'd save that particular pleasure for another day. But he vowed that pretty soon he'd pay Alexander a *proper* visit, reminisce about old times.

'You coming, Jack?' Gwen called, looking quizzically back over her shoulder.

'Coming,' Jack confirmed, and hurried to join her.

Five days later, Jack and Gwen were standing in the shadows of a yew tree in the drizzle of a cold Cardiff morning, watching as a pitiful straggle of mourners trudged away from a freshly dug grave with a black marble headstone.

'Didn't have many friends, did he?' Gwen said sadly.

'At least his mom loved him,' said Jack, indicating a sobbing woman being comforted by a grey-bearded man in a black coat.

When the mourners had departed, Jack and Gwen emerged and walked slowly across to the grave. The ground squelched beneath Gwen's feet. The sky overhead was a sinewy tangle of black and grey.

She knelt to place a posy of snowdrops against the headstone, and paused for a moment to contemplate the simple inscription beneath the name and dates: *My Beloved Son. Taken Too Soon.*

'The man who saved Cardiff,' Gwen murmured, straightening up. 'And no one will ever know.'

'Though if it hadn't been for Oscar, Cardiff wouldn't have needed saving in the first place,' Jack pointed out bluntly.

Gwen scowled. 'That was hardly his fault.'

'No,' said Jack. 'I guess not.'

They were silent for a moment. The chill breeze rippled through Gwen's hair and snatched at the tails of Jack's greatcoat.

'Wonder where the Dellacoi is now,' Gwen said eventually.

Jack shrugged. 'Found a way home, I hope. We're monitoring for energy readings, but… zilch.'

Gwen sighed. 'I really hope it doesn't turn up again.'

'Me too,' said Jack. 'That kind of virtual reality I can do without.'

Gwen smiled and took his hand. 'Come on, let's go.'

Together they trudged down the gentle incline towards the cemetery gates. Behind them the rising breeze plucked at the flowers on Oscar's grave, snatching up delicate white petals, which swirled away on the wind.

ACKNOWLEDGEMENTS

Big thanks to Sarah and Guy, Steve and Gary, and as ever to Nel, David and Polly, my wonderful, supportive family.

T O R C H W O O D
THE ENCYCLOPEDIA

ISBN 978 1 846 07764 7
£14.99

Founded by Queen Victoria in 1879, the Torchwood Institute has been defending Great Britain from the alien hordes for 130 years. Though London's Torchwood One was destroyed during the Battle of Canary Wharf, the small team at Torchwood Three have continued to monitor the space-time Rift that runs through Cardiff, saving the world and battling for the future of the human race.

Now you can discover every fact and figure, explore every crack in time and encounter every creature that Torchwood have dealt with. Included here are details of:

- The secret of the Children of Earth

- Operatives from Alice Guppy to Gwen Cooper

- Extraterrestrial visitors from Arcateenians to Weevils

- The life and deaths of Captain Jack Harkness

and much more. Illustrated throughout with photos and artwork from all three series, this A–Z provides everything you need to know about Torchwood.

Based on the hit series created by Russell T Davies for BBC Television.

Thick black clouds are blotting out the skies over Cardiff. As twenty-four inches of rain fall in twenty-four hours, the city centre's drainage system collapses. The capital's homeless are being murdered, their mutilated bodies left lying in the soaked streets around the Blaidd Drwg nuclear facility.

Tracked down by Torchwood, the killer calmly drops eight storeys to his death. But the killings don't stop. Their investigations lead Jack Harkness, Gwen Cooper and Toshiko Sato to a monster in a bathroom, a mystery at an army base and a hunt for stolen nuclear fuel rods. Meanwhile, Owen Harper goes missing from the Hub, when a game in *Second Reality* leads him to an old girlfriend…

Something is coming, forcing its way through the Rift, straight into Cardiff Bay.

Featuring Captain Jack Harkness as played by John Barrowman, with Gwen Cooper, Owen Harper, Toshiko Sato and Ianto Jones as played by Eve Myles, Burn Gorman, Naoki Mori and Gareth David-Lloyd, in the hit series created by Russell T Davies for BBC Television.

Also available from BBC Books

TORCHWOOD
BORDER PRINCES
Dan Abnett

ISBN 978 0 563 48654 1
£6.99

The End of the World began on a Thursday night in October, just after eight in the evening…

The Amok is driving people out of their minds, turning them into zombies and causing riots in the streets. A solitary diner leaves a Cardiff restaurant, his mission to protect the Principal leading him to a secret base beneath a water tower. Everyone has a headache, there's something in Davey Morgan's shed, and the church of St Mary-in-the-Dust, demolished in 1840, has reappeared – though it's not due until 2011. Torchwood seem to be out of their depth. What will all this mean for the romance between Torchwood's newest members?

Captain Jack Harkness has something more to worry about: an alarm, an early warning, given to mankind and held – inert – by Torchwood for 108 years. And now it's flashing. Something is coming. Or something is already here.

Featuring Captain Jack Harkness as played by John Barrowman, with Gwen Cooper, Owen Harper, Toshiko Sato and Ianto Jones as played by Eve Myles, Burn Gorman, Naoki Mori and Gareth David-Lloyd, in the hit series created by Russell T Davies for BBC Television.

Also available from BBC Books

TORCHWOOD
SLOW DECAY
Andy Lane

ISBN 978 0 563 48655 8
£6.99

When Torchwood track an energy surge to a Cardiff nightclub, the team finds the police are already at the scene. Five teenagers have died in a fight, and lying among the bodies is an unfamiliar device. Next morning, they discover the corpse of a Weevil, its face and neck eaten away, seemingly by human teeth. And on the streets of Cardiff, an ordinary woman with an extraordinary hunger is attacking people and eating her victims.

The job of a lifetime it might be, but working for Torchwood is putting big strains on Gwen's relationship with Rhys. While she decides to spice up their love life with the help of alien technology, Rhys decides it's time to sort himself out – better music, healthier food, lose some weight. Luckily, a friend has mentioned Doctor Scotus's weight-loss clinic…

Featuring Captain Jack Harkness as played by John Barrowman, with Gwen Cooper, Owen Harper, Toshiko Sato and Ianto Jones as played by Eve Myles, Burn Gorman, Naoki Mori and Gareth David-Lloyd, in the hit series created by Russell T Davies for BBC Television.

TORCHWOOD
SOMETHING IN THE WATER
Trevor Baxendale

ISBN 978 1 84607 437 0
£6.99

Dr Bob Strong's GP surgery has been treating a lot of coughs and colds recently, far more than is normal for the time of year. Bob thinks there's something up but he can't think what. He seems to have caught it himself, whatever it is – he's starting to cough badly and there are flecks of blood in his hanky.

Saskia Harden has been found on a number of occasions submerged in ponds or canals but alive and seemingly none the worse for wear. Saskia is not on any files, except in the medical records at Dr Strong's GP practice.

But Torchwood's priorities lie elsewhere: investigating ghostly apparitions in South Wales, they have found a dead body. It's old and in an advanced state of decay. And it is still able to talk.

And what it is saying is 'Water hag'…

Featuring Captain Jack Harkness as played by John Barrowman, with Gwen Cooper, Owen Harper, Toshiko Sato and Ianto Jones as played by Eve Myles, Burn Gorman, Naoki Mori and Gareth David-Lloyd, in the hit series created by Russell T Davies for BBC Television.

TORCHWOOD
TRACE MEMORY
David Llewellyn

ISBN 978 1 84607 438 7
£6.99

Tiger Bay, Cardiff, 1953. A mysterious crate is brought into the docks on a Scandinavian cargo ship. Its destination: the Torchwood Institute. As the crate is offloaded by a group of local dockers, it explodes, killing all but one of them, a young Butetown lad called Michael Bellini.

Fifty-five years later, a radioactive source somewhere inside the Hub leads Torchwood to discover the same Michael Bellini, still young and dressed in his 1950s clothes, cowering in the vaults. They soon realise that each has encountered Michael before – as a child in Osaka, as a junior doctor, as a young police constable, as a new recruit to Torchwood One. But it's Jack who remembers him best of all.

Michael's involuntary time-travelling has something to do with a radiation-charged relic held inside the crate. And the Men in Bowler Hats are coming to get it back.

Featuring Captain Jack Harkness as played by John Barrowman, with Gwen Cooper, Owen Harper, Toshiko Sato and Ianto Jones as played by Eve Myles, Burn Gorman, Naoki Mori and Gareth David-Lloyd, in the hit series created by Russell T Davies for BBC Television.

There's a part of the city that no one much goes to, a collection of rundown old houses and gloomy streets. No one stays there long, and no one can explain why – something's not quite right there.

Now the Council is renovating the district, and a new company is overseeing the work. There will be street parties and events to show off the newly gentrified neighbourhood: clowns and face-painters for the kids, magicians for the adults – the street entertainers of Cardiff, out in force.

None of this is Torchwood's problem. Until Toshiko recognises the sponsor of the street parties: Bilis Manger.

Now there is something for Torchwood to investigate. But Captain Jack Harkness has never been able to get into the area; it makes him physically ill to go near it. Without Jack's help, Torchwood must face the darker side of urban Cardiff alone…

Featuring Captain Jack Harkness as played by John Barrowman, with Gwen Cooper, Owen Harper, Toshiko Sato and Ianto Jones as played by Eve Myles, Burn Gorman, Naoki Mori and Gareth David-Lloyd, in the hit series created by Russell T Davies for BBC Television.

Also available from BBC Books

TORCHWOOD
PACK ANIMALS
Peter Anghelides

ISBN 978 1 846 07574 2
£6.99

Shopping for wedding gifts is enjoyable, unless like Gwen you witness a Weevil massacre in the shopping centre. A trip to the zoo is a great day out, until a date goes tragically wrong and Ianto is badly injured by stolen alien tech. And Halloween is a day of fun and frights, before unspeakable monsters invade the streets of Cardiff and it's no longer a trick or a treat for the terrified population.

Torchwood can control small groups of scavengers, but now someone has given large numbers of predators a season ticket to Earth. Jack's investigation is hampered when he finds he's being investigated himself. Owen is convinced that it's just one guy who's toying with them. But will Torchwood find out before it's too late that the game is horribly real, and the deck is stacked against them?

Featuring Captain Jack Harkness as played by John Barrowman, with Gwen Cooper, Owen Harper, Toshiko Sato and Ianto Jones as played by Eve Myles, Burn Gorman, Naoki Mori and Gareth David-Lloyd, in the hit series created by Russell T Davies for BBC Television.

Also available from BBC Books

T O R C H W O O D
SKYPOINT
Phil Ford

ISBN 978 1 846 07575 9
£6.99

'If you're going to be anyone in Cardiff, you're going to be at SkyPoint!'

SkyPoint is the latest high-rise addition to the ever-developing Cardiff skyline. It's the most high-tech, avant-garde apartment block in the city. And it's where Rhys Williams is hoping to find a new home for himself and Gwen. Gwen's more concerned by the money behind the tower block – Besnik Lucca, a name she knows from her days in uniform.

When Torchwood discover that residents have been going missing from the tower block, one of the team gets her dream assignment. Soon SkyPoint's latest newly married tenants are moving in. And Toshiko Sato finally gets to make a home with Owen Harper.

Then something comes out of the wall...

Featuring Captain Jack Harkness as played by John Barrowman, with Gwen Cooper, Owen Harper, Toshiko Sato and Ianto Jones as played by Eve Myles, Burn Gorman, Naoki Mori and Gareth David-Lloyd, in the hit series created by Russell T Davies for BBC Television.

T O R C H W O O D
ALMOST PERFECT
James Goss

ISBN 978 1 846 07573 5
£6.99

Emma is 30, single and frankly desperate. She woke up this morning with nothing to look forward to but another evening of unsuccessful speed-dating. But now she has a new weapon in her quest for Mr Right. And it's made her almost perfect.

Gwen Cooper woke up this morning expecting the unexpected. As usual. She went to work and found a skeleton at a table for two and a colleague in a surprisingly glamorous dress. Perfect.

Ianto Jones woke up this morning with no memory of last night. He went to work, where he caused amusement, suspicion and a little bit of jealousy. Because Ianto Jones woke up this morning in the body of a woman. And he's looking just about perfect.

Jack Harkness has always had his doubts about Perfection.

Featuring Captain Jack Harkness as played by John Barrowman, with Gwen Cooper and Ianto Jones as played by Eve Myles and Gareth David-Lloyd, in the hit series created by Russell T Davies for BBC Television.

Also available from BBC Books

T O R C H W O O D
INTO THE SILENCE
Sarah Pinborough

ISBN 978 1 846 07753 1
£6.99

The body in the church hall is very definitely dead. It has been sliced open with surgical precision, its organs exposed, and its vocal cords are gone. It is as if they were never there or they've been dissolved…

With the Welsh Amateur Operatic Contest getting under way, music is filling the churches and concert halls of Cardiff. The competition has attracted the finest Welsh talent to the city, but it has also drawn something else – there are stories of a metallic creature hiding in the shadows. Torchwood are on its tail, but it's moving too fast for them to track it down.

This new threat requires a new tactic – so Ianto Jones is joining a male voice choir…

Featuring Captain Jack Harkness as played by John Barrowman, with Gwen Cooper and Ianto Jones as played by Eve Myles and Gareth David-Lloyd, in the hit series created by Russell T Davies for BBC Television.

Also available from BBC Books

T O R C H W O O D
THE HOUSE THAT JACK BUILT
Guy Adams

ISBN 978 1 846 07739 5
£6.99

Jackson Leaves – an Edwardian house in Penylan, built 1906, semi-detached, three storeys, spacious, beautifully presented. Left in good condition to Rob and Julia by Rob's late aunt.

It's an ordinary sort of a house. Except for the way the rooms don't stay in the same places. And the strange man that turns up in the airing cupboard. And the apparitions. And the temporal surges that attract the attentions of Torchwood.

And the fact that the first owner of Jackson Leaves in 1906 was a Captain Jack Harkness…

Featuring Captain Jack Harkness as played by John Barrowman, with Gwen Cooper and Ianto Jones as played by Eve Myles and Gareth David-Lloyd, in the hit series created by Russell T Davies for BBC Television.

TORCHWOOD
THE UNDERTAKER'S GIFT
Trevor Baxendale

ISBN 978 1 846 07782 1
£6.99

The Hokrala Corp lawyers are back. They're suing planet Earth for mishandling the twenty-first century, and they won't tolerate any efforts to repel them. An assassin has been sent to remove Captain Jack Harkness.

It's been a busy week in Cardiff. The Hub's latest guest is a translucent, amber jelly carrying a lethal electrical charge. Record numbers of aliens have been coming through the Rift, and Torchwood could do without any more problems.

But there are reports of an extraordinary funeral cortege in the night-time city, with mysterious pallbearers guarding a rotting cadaver that simply doesn't want to be buried.

Torchwood should be ready for anything – but with Jack the target of an invisible killer, Gwen trapped in a forgotten crypt and Ianto Jones falling desperately ill, could a world of suffering be the Undertaker's gift to planet Earth?

Featuring Captain Jack Harkness as played by John Barrowman, with Gwen Cooper and Ianto Jones as played by Eve Myles and Gareth David-Lloyd, in the hit series created by Russell T Davies for BBC Television.

T O R C H W O O D
RISK ASSESSMENT
James Goss

ISBN 978 1 846 07783 8
£6.99

'Are you trying to tell me, Captain Harkness, that the entire staff of Torchwood Cardiff now consists of yourself, a woman in trousers and a tea boy?'

Agnes Haversham is awake, and Jack is worried (and not a little afraid). The Torchwood Assessor is roused from her deep sleep in only the worst of times – it's happened just four times in the last 100 years. Can the situation really be so bad?

Someone, somewhere, is fighting a war, and they're losing badly. The coffins of the dead are coming through the Rift. With thousands of alien bodies floating in the Bristol Channel, it's down to Torchwood to round them all up before a lethal plague breaks out.

And now they'll have to do it by the book. The 1901 edition.

Featuring Captain Jack Harkness as played by John Barrowman, with Gwen Cooper and Ianto Jones as played by Eve Myles and Gareth David-Lloyd, in the hit series created by Russell T Davies for BBC Television.

Coming soon from BBC Books

TORCHWOOD
CONSEQUENCES

ISBN 978 1 846 07784 5
£6.99

Saving the planet, watching over the Rift, preparing the human race for the twenty-first century... Torchwood has been keeping Cardiff safe since the late 1800s. Small teams of heroes, working 24/7, encountering and containing the alien, the bizarre and the inexplicable.

But Torchwood do not always see the effects of their actions. What links the Rules and Regulations for replacing a Torchwood leader to the destruction of a shopping centre? How does a witness to an alien's reprisals against Torchwood become caught up in a night of terror in a university library? And why should Gwen and Ianto's actions at a local publishers have a cost for Torchwood more than half a century earlier?

For Torchwood, the past will always catch up with them. And sometimes the future will catch up with the past...

Featuring stories by writers for the hit series created by Russell T Davies for BBC Television, including Joseph Lidster and James Moran, plus Andrew Cartmel, David Llewellyn and Sarah Pinborough.